James Sheridan Knowles

The love-chase

A comedy in five acts

James Sheridan Knowles

The love-chase
A comedy in five acts

ISBN/EAN: 9783337252151

Printed in Europe, USA, Canada, Australia, Japan

Cover: Foto ©Andreas Hilbeck / pixelio.de

More available books at **www.hansebooks.com**

No. XXII.

FRENCH'S STANDARD DRAMA.

———◆———

THE LOVE-CHASE.

𝔄 Comedy

IN FIVE ACTS.

BY JAMES SHERIDAN KNOWLES.

WITH THE STAGE BUSINESS, CAST OF CHARACTERS COS
UMES, RELATIVE POSITIONS, &c.

AS PLAYED AT THE PARK THEATRE,

———◆◆◆———

NEW YORK :
Samuel French & Son,
PUBLISHERS,
No. 122 Nassau Street.

LONDON .
Samuel French,
PUBLISHER,
89 STRAND.

CAST OF CHARACTERS,

As originally played at the Drury Lane and Park Theatres.

	Drury Lane.	Paris.
Sir William Fondlove (an old Baronet)..	Mr. Strickland.	Mr. Placide.
Waller (in love with Lydia)............	" Elton.	" Wheatly.
Wildrake (a Sportsman)...............	" Webster.	" Mason.
Trueworth (a friend of Sir William)....	" Hemmings.	" Fredericks.
Neville, }Friends to Waller	" Woorel.	' Nexsen.
Humphries, }	" Hutchings.	" Wells.
Lash...............................	" Ross.	" Johnson.
Chargewell	" Edwards.	" Povey.
George	" Bishop.	" Gallot.
Servant		" Garland.
Lawyer	" Ray.	" King.
Widow Green......................	Mrs. Glover.	Mrs. Wheatley
Constance (daughter to Sir William) ...	Mrs. Nisbett.	" Shaw.
Lydia................................	Miss Vandenhoff	" Richardson
Alice................................	Mrs. Tayleure.	" Durie.
Phœbe	Miss Wrighten.	" Conway.
Amelia.............................	" Gallot.	Miss Verity.

Four Bridesmen, Three Bridesmaids, and Three Servants

COSTUMES.

SIR WILLIAM FONDLOVE.—Black and gold costume of Charles II.—Second dress· do. of white and silver.
WALLER.—Light brown dress, edged with scarlet.
WILDRAKE.—Dark brown dress and high bonts.
TRUEWORTH.—Dress of black velvet with scarlet puffs.
NEVILLE and HUMPHREYS.—Dark brown, edged with black.
LASH.—Russet-coloured jerkin.
CHARGEWELL.—Dark brown dress and green apron.
GEORGE.—Buff jerkin.
SERVANT—Ditto.
LAWYERS.—Black with black gown.
FOUR BRIDESMEN.—White satin and silver.
THREE SERVANTS.—Buff jerkins.
WIDOW GREEN.—Grey and black dress with points and beads.
CONSTANCE.—Dress of rose-coloured satin.—Second dress: scarlet riding habit. —Third dress: White satin and flowers.
LYDIA.—Plain brown dress with black body.—Second dress, of white satin and silver, and wedding veil.
ALICE—Dark brown dress and point lace
PHŒBE.—Grey dress with black points.
AMELIA.—White satin and silver.
BRIDESMAIDS.—White satin and silver.

EXITS AND ENTRANCES.

R. means *Right*; L. *Left*; R. D. *Right Door*; L. D. *Left Door*; S. E. *Second Entrance*; U. E. *Upper Entrance*; M. D. *Middle Door*

RELATIVE POSITIONS.

R., means *Right*; L., *Left*; C., *Centre*; R. C., *Right of Centre* L. C., *Left of Centre.*

N.B. *Passages marked with* Inverted Commas, *are usually omitted in the representation.*

EDITORIAL INTRODUCT ON.

THE title, plot, and characters of this comedy, are among the author's most felicitous conceptions. "The Love Chase" was originally produced the ninth of October, 1837, at the Haymarket Theatre, London. Its success was unequivocal. Mrs. Nisbet, as *Constance*, won the greatest share of the laurels bestowed upon the performers on the occasion. "She caught," says one of the critics of the day, "the full meaning of this finely drawn part, and conveyed its spirit to the audience with a fascinating power, which drew forth reiterated plaudits in every scene. Her delivery of the beautiful language, with which she was entrusted, was easy and natural, yet full of point, enforced by action characteristically vigorous, but not unfeminine, and graceful without the slightest degree of affectation. With regard to the merit of the play itself, the delight we experienced in witnessing the production of a comedy, which displays much of the beauty and power of our early dramatists, without a particle of their grossness, renders the task of fault-finding difficult and disagreeable."

In America, "The Love Chase" has been always an acceptable play to audiences, though it has not attained the popularity of "The Hunchback" or "The Wife." Some of the stage situations are very cleverly contrived. That wherein the *Widow Green* thinks she has excited the jealousy of *Master Waller* while encouraging the addresses of *Sir William Fondlove*, never fails to be highly amusing when well presented; and the contrivance by which *Wildrake* is roused to woo "*Neighbour Constance*," and *Constance* is, on her part, alarmed at the idea of losing "*Neighbour Wildrake*," is ingenious and effective. True there is some little violation of the probabilities of real life, in

Constance's undetected disguise; but we can almost forget this as a fault, when we recollect it has afforded the author an opportunity of introducing the spirited description of the chase, which he puts into the mouth of his heroine—a description which has been lamely imitated in a recent comedy, professing to depict English fashionable society.

The contrast in the characters of " *Lydia*" and " *Constance,* ' is dramatically conceived; but we are at a loss to know *why* the former should have been attacked by ruffians at the precise moment she is on her way to her lover's house. To make a deed dramatic, we must see that it has a sufficient motive. This is wanting in the instance we allude to; and the consequence is, that *Lydia* utterly lacks our sympathy when she is brought in exanimate from terror. We see at once, that she has been attacked solely for the author's convenience, and not because it was in the nature of occurrences that an attack should be made.

This play is by no means deficient in beauties of language and thought. One of the most admirable specimens of word-painting that we remember, is *Sir William Fondlove's* description of the *Widow Green*, in the first act. There she is, vividly before us, as we read. We can see her entering a drawing-room, or presiding at the card-table. We want no illustration by Cruikshank or Browne, to show us how she looks. Her well-rounded figure, her dimples, her air and manner, the very tones of her voice, are so inimitably pourtrayed by the author, that we ask no limner's skill to aid us in forming an adequate conception of the character.

The concluding scene of the " Love Chase" bears marks of haste and negligence. *Constance* should have had the last speech. The words spoken by the *Widow*, have been justly complained of as tame and obscure. But notwithstanding this and other flaws in the execution, the comedy is one of the best and most unexceptionable of modern plays.

TO JOHN VANDENHOFF, ESQ

MY DEAR SIR,

It is to your suggestion and encouragement that I owe this return o Dramatic Composition. Your taste and judgment have also assisted in the completion of the work; and to you I dedicate that which is in debted to you for its existence.

The value of the offering is very doubtful—but not the sincerity with which it is made—nor the estimation in which your talents are held, and your friendship prized, by

Your obliged and ever faithful servant,

THE AUTHOR.

———◆———

AUTHOR'S PREFACE.

PREFACES are generally tedious things—troublesome to the writer, wearying to the reader, and perhaps in most cases better omitted alto-gether. Yet a little mercy may fairly be craved by an author who, on the eve of the production of his work, finds himself nearly a thousand miles away from the scene of his interests—unable to correct any of the faults which a nearer view might have rendered visible to him—and beyond the reach of even a single proof sheet.

Such is the position of the writer of the following pages; and his fate will be decided long before it can be known to himself. He is, however, fortunate in the support of talents for his principal charac-ters, which he knows will more than work out his own conceptions. To these and to an indulgent Public, whose kindness he has more than once experienced, he commits himself.

. Some resemblance will be found between the conduct of a portion of this play, and Mr. James's novel of the *Ancien Regime*. That gentleman's lamp, however, is too bright for him to grudge a little of its light to one whose own taper burns more dully.

Breslau, August, 1842.

THE LOVE·CHASE

ACT I.

SCENE I.—*The Lobby of an Inn.*

Enter CHARGEWELL, *hurriedly,* L.

Char. WHAT, hoa, there! Hoa, Sirrahs! More wine!
Are the knaves asleep? Let not our guests cool, or we
shall starve the till! Good waiting, more than viands and
wine, doth help to make the Inn! George!—Richard!
—Ralph!—Where are you?

Enter GEORGE, R.

Geo. Here am I, Sir.
Char. Have they taken in more wine to that company?
Geo. Yes, Sir.
Char. That's right. Serve them as quick as they order!
A fair company! I have seen them here before. Take
care they come again. A choice company! That Master
Waller, I hear, is a fine spirit—leads the town. Pay him
much duty. A deep purse, and easy strings!
Geo. And there is another, Sir;—a capital gentleman,
though from the country. A gentleman most learned in
dogs and horses! He doth talk wondrous edification:—
one Master Wildrake. I wish you could hear him, Sir.
Char. Well, well!—attend to them. Let them not cool
o er the liquor, or their calls will grow slack. Keep feed
ing the fire while it blazes, and the blaze will continue.
Look to it well!
Geo. I will, Sir.

Char. And be careful, above all, that you please Master Waller. He is a guest worth pleasing ; he is a gentleman.—Free order, quick pay !

Geo. And such, I'll dare be sworn, is the other. A man of mighty stores of knowledge—most learned in dogs and horses ! Never was I so edified by the discourse of mortal man. [*Exeunt, Chargewell,* L., *George,* R.

Scene II.—*A Room in an Inn.*

Masters Waller, Wildrake, Trueworth. Neville, *and* Humphreys, *sitting round a table,* c.

Wal. Well, Master Wildrake, speak you of the chase !
To hear you, one doth feel the bounding steed ;
You bring the hounds, and game, and all to view—
All scudding to the jovial huntsman's cheer !
And yet I pity the poor crownéd deer,
And always fancy 'tis by Fortune's spite,
That lordly head of his, he bears so high—
Like Virtue, stately in calamity,
And hunted by the human, worldly hound—
Is made to fly before the pack, that straight
Burst into song at prospect of his death
You say their cry is harmony ; and yet
The chorus scarce is music to my ear,
When I bethink me what it sounds to his ;
Nor deem I sweet the note that rings the knell
Of the once merry forester !
Nev. The same things
Do please or pain, according to the thought
We take of them. Some smile at their own death,
Which most do shrink from, as a beast of prey
It kills to look upon. But you, who take
Such pity of the deer, whence follows it
You hunt more costly game ?—The comely maid,
To wit, that waits on buxom Widow Green ?
Hum. The comely maid !—Such term not half the sum
Of her rich beauty gives ! Were rule to go
By loveliness, I know not in the court,
Or city, lady might not fitly serve
That lady serving-maid !
True. Come ! your defence !

Why show you ruth where there's least argument,
Deny it where there's most ?　You will not plead !
Oh, Master Waller, where we use to hunt,
We think the sport no crime.

　Hum. I give you joy,
You prosper in your chase.

　Wal. Not so !　The maid
In simple honesty I must pronounce
A miracle of virtue, well as beauty.

　Nev. And well do I believe you, Master Waller ;
Those know I who have ventured gift and promise
But for a minute of her ear—the boon
Of a poor dozen words spoke through a chink—
And come off bootless, save the haughty scorn
That cast their bounties back to them again.

　True. That warrants her what Master Waller speaks her
Is she so very fair ?

　Nev. Yes, Master Trueworth ;
And I believe indeed an honest maid ;
But love's the coin to market with for love,
And that knows Master Waller.　On pretence
Of sneaking kindness for gay Widow Green,
He visits her for sake of her fair maid !
To whom a glance or word avails to hint
His proper errand : and—as glimpses only
Do only serve to whet the wish to see—
Awakens interest to hear the tale
So stintingly that's told.　I know his practice—
Luck to you, Master Waller !　If you win,
You merit it, who take the way to win !

　Wal. Good, Master Neville !

　True. I should laugh to see
The poacher snared !—the maid, for mistress sought,
Turn out a wife.

　Nev. How say you, Master Waller ?
Things quite as strange have fallen !

　Wal. Impossible !

　True. Impossible !　Most possible of things—
If thou'rt in love !　Where merit lies itself,
What matters it to want the name, which, weighed,
Is not the worth of so much breath as it takes
To utter it !　" If but from Nature's hand,

" She is all you could expect of gentle blood,
" Face, form, mien, speech ; with these, what to belong
" To lady more behoves—thoughts delicate,
" Affections generous, and modesty—
" Perfectionating, brightening crown of all !—-
'' If she hath these—true titles to thy heart—
* What doth she lack that's title to thy hand ?
* The name of lady, which is none of these,
" But may belong without ?"   Thou might'st do worse
Than marry her !   Thou would'st, undoing her !
Yea, by my mother's name, a shameful act,
Most shamefully performed !
    Wal. [*Starting up and drawing*, R. C.) Sir !
    Nev. [*And the others interposing*, C.) Gentlemen !
    True. (L. C.) All's right !   Sit down !—I will not draw
      again.
A word with you :—If—as a man—thou say'st,
Upon thy honour, I have spoken wrong,
I'll ask thy pardon—though I never hold
Communion with thee more !
    Wal. [*After a pause, putting up his sword*, R. C.) My
      sword is sheathed !
Wilt let me take thy hand ?
    True. (L. C.) 'Tis thine, good Sir,
And faster than before—A fault confessed,
Is a new virtue added to a man !
" Yet let me own some blame was mine.   A truth
" May be too harshly told"—but 'tis a theme
I am tender on—I had a sister, Sir—
You understand me !—'Twas my happiness
To own her once—I would forget her now !--
I have forgotten !—I know not if she lives !—
Things of such strain as we were speaking of,
Spite of myself, remind me of her !—So !—
    Nev. Sit down !   Let's have more wine.
    Wild. (L.) Not so, good Sirs.
Partaking of your hospitality,
I have overlooked good friends I came to visit,
And who have late become sojourners here—
Old country friends and neighbors, and with whom
I e'en take up my quarters.   Master Trueworth,
Bear witness for me.

True. It is even so :
Sir William Fondlove and his charming daughter.
    Wild. Ay, neighbour Constance. Charming, does he
        say ?
Yes, neighbour Constance is a charming girl
To those that do not know her.   If she plies me
As hard as was her custom in the country,
I should not wonder, though this very day
I seek tne home I quitted for a month !   [*Aside,* R.
Good even, gentlemen.   [*Crosses,* L., *going out.*
    Hum. Nay, if you go,
We all break up, and sally forth together.
    Wal. (R. C.) Be it so—Your hand again, good Master
        Trueworth !
I am sorry I did pain you
    True. (C.) It is thine, Sir.   [*They go out,* L

SCENE III.—*Sir William Fondlove's House.—A Room.*

Enter SIR WILLIAM, R.

Sir W. At sixty-two, to be in leading strings,
Is an old child—and with a daughter, too !
Her mother held me ne'er in check so strait
As she.   I must not go but where she likes,
Nor see but whom she likes, do anything
But what she likes !—A slut, bare twenty-one !
Nor minces she commands !—A brigadier
More coolly doth not give his orders out
Than she !   Her waiting maid is aid-de-camp ;
My steward adjutant ; my lacqueys sergeants ;
That bring me her high pleasure how I march
And counter-march—when I'm on duty—when
I'm off—when suits it not to tell it me
Herself—" Sir William, thus my mistress says !"
As saying it were enongh—no will of mine
Consulted !   I will marry.   Must I serve,   ‑
Better a wife, my mistress, than a daughter !
And yet the vixen says, if I do marry,
I'll find she'll rule my wife as well as me !

Enter TRUEWORTH, L.

Ah, Master Trueworth !   Welcome, Master Trueworth !

True. Thanks, Sir ; I am glad to see you look so well !

Sir W. Ah, Master Trueworth, when one turns the hill,
'Tis rapid going down !   We climb by steps ;
By strides, we reach the bottom.   Look at me,
And guess my age.

True. Turned fifty.

Sir W. Ten years more !
How marvellously well I wear !   I think
You would not flatter me !—But scan me close,
And pryingly, as one who seeks a thing
He means to find—What signs of age dost see ?

True. None !

Sir W. None about the corners of the eyes ?
Lines that diverge like to the spider's joists,
Whereon he builds his airy fortalice ?
They call them crow's feet—has the ugly bird
Been perching there ?—Eh ?—Well ?

True. There's something like,
But not what one must see, unless he's blind
Like steeple on a hill.

Sir W. [*After a pause.*] Your eyes are good !
I am certainly a wonder for my age ;
I walk as well as ever !   Do I stoop ?

True. A plummet from your head would find your heel.

Sir W. It is my make—my make, good Master True-
   worth ;
I do not study it.   Do you observe
The hollow in my back ?   That's natural.
As now I stand, so stood I when a child,
A rosy, chubby boy !—I am youthful to
A miracle !   My arm is firm as 'twas
At twenty.   Feel it !

True. [*Feeling his arm.*] It is deal !

Sir W. Oak—oak,
Isn't it, Master Trueworth ?   Thou hast known me
Ten years and upwards.   Think'st my leg is shrunk ?

True. No.

Sir W. No ! not in the calf ?

True. As big a calf
As ever.

Sir W. Thank you, thank you—I believe it !
When others waste 'tis growing time with me !

I feel it, Master Trueworth! Vigour, Sir,
In every joint of me!—could run! could leap!
Why shouldn't I marry? Knife and fork I play
Better than many a boy of twenty-five—
Why shouldn't I marry? If they come to wine,
My brace of bottles can I carry home,
And ne'er a headache. Death! why shouldn't I marry?
　True. I see in nature no impediment.
　Sir W. Impediment? she's all appliances!—
And fortune's with me, too! The Widow Green
Gives hints to me! The pleasant Widow Green!
Whose fortieth year, instead of autumn, brings
A second Summer in. Odds boddikins,
How young she looks! What life is in her eyes!
What ease is in her gait! while, as she walks,
Her waist, still tapering, takes it pliantly!
How lollingly she bears her head withal:
On this side now—now that! When enters she
A drawing-room, what worlds of gracious things
Her courtesy says!—she sinks with such a sway,
Greeting on either hand the company,
Then slowly rises to her state again!
She is the empress of the card-table!
Her hand and arm!—Gods, did you see her deal—
With curved and pliant wrist dispense the pack,
Which at the touch of her fair fingers fly!
How soft she speaks—how very soft! Her voice
Comes melting-from her round and swelling throat,
Reminding you of sweetest, mellowest things—
Plums, peaches, apricots and nectarines—
Whose bloom is poor to paint her cheeks and lips.
By Jove, I'll marry!　　　　　　　　[*Crosses,* L
　True. You forget, Sir William,
I do not know the lady.
　Sir W. Great your loss.
By all the Gods, I'll marry!—But my daughter
Must needs be married first. She rules my house;
Would rule it still. and will not have me wed.
A clever, handsome, darling, forward minx!
When I became a widower, the reins
Her mother dropped she caught,—a hoyden girl;
Nor since would e'er give up, howe'er I strove

B

To coax or catch them from her.   One way still
Or t'other, she would keep them—laugh, pout, plead;
Now vanquish me with water, now with fire;
Would box my face, and, ere I well could ope
My mouth to chide her, stop it with a kiss!
The monkey! what a plague she's to me!—How
I love her! how I love the Widow Green!   [*Crosses*, R.

    True. Then marry her!

    Sir W. I tell thee, first of all
Must needs my daughter marry.—See I not
A hope of that; she naught affects the sex:
Comes suitor after suitor—all in vain.
Fast as they bow, she courtesies, and says " Nay!"
Or she, a woman, lacks a woman's heart,
Or hath a special taste which none can hit. ·

    True. Or taste, perhaps, which is already hit.

    Sir W. Eh!—how?

    True. Remember you no country friend,
Companion of her walks—her squire to church,
Her beau whenever she went visiting—
Before she came to town?

    Sir W. No!

    True. None?—art sure?
No playmate when she was a girl?

    Sir W. Oh! ay!
That Master Wildrake I did pray thee go
And wait for at the Inn, but had forgotten.
Is he come?

    True. And in the house.—Some friends that met him,
As he alighted, laid strong hands upon him
And made him stop for dinner.   We had else
Been earlier with you.

    Sir W. Ha!   I am glad he's come.

    True. She may be smit with him.

    Sir W. As cat with dog!

    True. He heard her voice as we did mount the stairs,
And darted straight to join her.

    Sir W. You shall see
What wondrous calm and harmony take place,
When fire meets gunpowder!

    Con. [*Without*, R.) Who sent for you?
What made you come?

Wild. [*Without*, R.) To see the town, not you !—
A kiss !
Con. I vow I'll not.
Wild. I swear you shall.
Con. A saucy cub !   I vow, I had as lieve
Your whipper-in had kissed me !
Sir W. Do you hear ?
True. I do.   Most pleasing discords !

        Enter CONSTANCE *and* WILDRAKE, R.

Con. Father, speak
To neighbour Wildrake.
Sir W. Very glad to see him.
Wild. I thank you, good Sir William !   Give you joy
Of your good looks !
Con. What, Phœbe !—Phœbe !—Phœbe !
Sir W. What want'st thou with thy lap-dog ?
Con. Only, Sir,
To welcome neighbor Wildrake !   What a figure
To shew himself in town !
Sir W. Wilt hold thy peace ?
Con. Yes ; if you'll lesson me to hold my laughter.
Wildrake !
Wild. Well ?
Con. Let me walk thee in the Park—
How they would stare at thee !
Sir W. Wilt ne'er give o'er ?
Wild. Nay, let her have her way—I heed her not !
Though to more courteous welcome I have right ;
Although I am neighbour Wildrake !   Reason is reason !
   Con. And right is right ! so welcome, neighbour Wild- -
        rake,
I am very, very, very glad to see you !
Come, for a quarter of an hour, we'll e'en
Agree together !—How do your horses, neighbour ?
   Wild. Pshaw !
   Con. And your dogs ?
   Wild. Pshaw !
   Con. Whipper-in and huntsman ?
   Sir W. Converse of things thou know'st to talk about
   Con. And keep him silent, father, when I know
He cannot talk of any other things ?

How does thy hunter?   What a sorry trick
He played thee t'other day, to balk his leap,
And throw thee, neighbour!   Did he balk the leap?
Confess!   You sportsmen never are to blame!
Say you are fowlers, 'tis your dog's in fault;
Say you are anglers, 'tis your tackle's wrong;
Say you are hunters, why, the honest horse
That bears your weight, must bear your blunders, too!
Why, whither go you?   •
   Wild. Any where from thee.
   Con. With me, you mean.
   Wild. I mean it not.
   Con. You do!
I'll give you fifty reasons for't—and first,
Where you go, neighbour, I'll go!
     [*They go out,* L.— *Wild. pettishly, Constance laugh* g
   Sir W. Do you mark?
Much love is there!
   True. Indeed, a heap, or none.
I'd wager on the heap!
   Sir W. Ay!—Do you think
These discords, as in the musician's art,
Are subtle servitors to harmony?
That all this war's for peace?   This wrangling but
A masquerade, where love his roguish face
Conceals beneath an ugly visor!—Well?
   True. Your guess and my conceit are not a mile
Apart.   " Unlike to other common flowers,
" The flower of love shows various in the bud,
" 'Twill look a thistle, and 'twill blow a rose!"
And with your leave, I'll put it to the test;
Affect myself, for thy fair daughter, love—
Make him my confidant—dilate to him
Upon the graces of her heart and mind,
Feature and form—that well may comment bear—
Till—" like the practised connoisseur, who finds
" A gem of art out in a household picture
" The unskilled owner held so cheap, he grudged
" Renewal of the chipped and tarnished frame,
' But values now as priceless—" I arouse him
Into a quick sense of the worth of that
" Whose merit hitherto from lack of skill,

" Or dulling habit of acquaintanceship,"
He has not been awake to.
   Con. [*Without,* c. D.] Neighbour Wildrake !
   Sir W. Hither they come. I fancy well thy game !
Oh, to be free to marry Widow Green !
I'll call her hence anon—then ply him well. [*Goes out,* R
   Wild. [*Without.*] Nay, neighbour Constance !
   True. He's high in storm.

      Enter WILDRAKE *and* CONSTANCE, L. D.

   Wild. To Lincolnshire, I tell thee.
   Con. Lincolnshire !
What, prithee, takes thee off to Lincolnshire.
   Wild. Too great delight in thy fair company.
   True. Nay, Master Wildrake, why away so soon ?
You 're scarce a day in town !—" Extremes like this,
" And starts of purpose, are the signs 'tis love,
" Though immatured as yet.   [*Aside.*'
   Con. He's long enough
In town ! What should he here ? He's lost in town :
No man is he for concerts, balls or routs !
No game he knows at cards, save rare Pope Joan !
He ne'er could master dance beyond a jig ;
And as for music, nothing to compare
To the melodious yelping of a hound,
Except the braying of his huntsman's horn !
Ask *him* to stay in town !
   Sir W. [*without,* R.) Hoa, Constance !
   Con. Sir !—
Neighbour, a pleasant ride to Lincolnshire !
Good bye !
   Sir W. [*without,* R.) Why, Constance !
   Con. Coming, Sir ! Shake hands !
Neighbour, good bye ! Don't look so wo-begone ;
'Tis but a two-days' ride, and thou wilt see
Rover, and Spot, and Nettle, and the rest
Of thy dear country friends !
   Sir W. [*without,* R.) Constance ! I say.
   Con. Anon !—Commend me to the gentle souls,
And pat them for me !—Will you, neighbour Wildrake !
   Sir W. *without,* R.) Why, Constance ! Constance !
   Con. In a moment, Sir !

Good bye!—I'd cry, dear nei,.hbour, if I could!
Good bye!—a pleasant day, when next you hunt!
And, prithee, mind thy horse don't balk his leap!
Good bye—and, after dinner, drink my health!
" A bumper, Sirs, to neighbour Constance!"—Do!—
And give it with a speech, wherein unfold
My many graces, more accomplishments,
And virtues topping either—in a word,
How I'm the fairest, kindest, best of neighbours!

    *[They go out severally.—Trueworth trying to pacify
      Wildrake,* L.*—Constance laughing,* R.

END OF ACT I.

ACT II.

Scene I.—*A Room in Sir William's House.*

Enter Trueworth *and* Wildrake, R.

  Wild. Nay, Master Trueworth, I must needs be gone!
She treats me worse and worse! I am a stock,
That words have none to pay her. For her sake,
I quit the town to-day. I like a jest,
But hers are jests past bearing. I am her butt
She nothing does but practise on! A plague!—
Fly her shafts ever your way?
  True. Would they did!
  Wild. Art mad?—or wishest she should drive thee so?
  True. Thou know'st her not.
  Wild. I know not neighbour Constance?
Then know I not myself, or anything
Which as myself I know!
  True. Heigh ho!
  Wild. Heigh ho!
Why, what a burden that for a man's song!
'Twould fit a maiden that was sick for love.
Heigh ho! Come, ride with me to Lincolnshire,
And turn thy " heigh ho!" into " hilly ho!"
  True. Nay, rather tarry thou in town with me.
Men sometimes find a friend's hand of avail,
When useless proves their own   Wilt 'end me thine?

Wild Or may my horse break down in a steeple chase!
True. A steeple chase! What made thee think of that?
I'm for the steeple—not to ride a race
Only to get there!—not alone, in sooth;
But in fair company!
    Wild. Thou'rt not in love!
    True. Heigh ho!
    Wild. Thou wouldst not marry!
    True. With your help.
    Wild. And whom, I prithee?
    True. Gentle mistress Constance!
    Wild. What!—neighbour Constance?—Never did I
     dream   .
That mortal man would fall in love with her.   [*Aside.*
In love with neighbour Constance?—I feel strange
At thought that she should marry!—[*Aside.*] Go to church
With neighbour Constance! That's a steeple chase
I never thought of. I feel very strange;
What seest in neighbour Constance?
    True. Lovers' eyes
See with a vision proper to themselves,
Yet thousand eyes will vouch what mine affirm.
First, then, I see in her the mould express
Of woman—stature, feature, body, limb—
Breathing the gentle sex we value most,
When most 'tis at antipodes with ours!
    Wild. You mean that neighbour Constance is a woman
Why, yes; she is a woman, certainly.
    True. So much for person. Now for her complexion.
What shall we liken to her dainty skin?
Her arm, for instance?—
    Wild. Snow will match it.
    True. Snow!—
It is her arm without the smoothness on't.
Then is not snow transparent. 'Twill not do.
    Wild. A pearl's transparent!
    True. So it is, but yet
Yields not elastic to the thrilléd touch!
I know not what to liken to her arm,
Except its beauteous fellow! Oh, to be
The chosen friend of two such neighbours!
    Wild Would

His tongue would made a halt. He makes too free
With neighbour Constance ! Can't he let her arms
Alone !   I trust their chosen friend
Will ne'er be he ! I'm vexed.   [*Aside*

  True. But graceful things
Grow doubly graceful in the graceful use !
Hast marked her ever walk the drawing-room ?
  Wild. [*Snappishly.*] No.
  True. No !   Why, where have been your eyes ?
  Wild. In my head !
But I begin to doubt if open yet.   [*Aside.*

  True. Yet that's a trifle to the dance : down which
She floats as though she were a form of air ;
" The ground feels not her foot, or tells not on't ;
" Her movements are the painting of the strain,
" Its swell, its fall, its mirth, its tenderness !
" Then is she fifty Constances ! each moment
" Another one, and each, except its fellow,
" Without a peer !"   You have danced with her ?
  Wild. I hate
To dance ! I can't endure to dance ! [*Crosses* L.] Of course
You have danced with her ?
  True. I have.
  Wild. You have ?
  True. I have.
  Wild. I do abominate to dance !—Could carve
Fiddlers and company ! A dancing man,
To me, was ever like a dancing dog !
Save less to be endured !—Ne'er saw I one,
But I bethought me of the master's whip.
  True. A man might bear the whip to dance with her !
  Wild. Not if I had the laying of it on !
  True. Well ; let that pass. The lady is the theme.
  Wild. Yes ; make an end of it !—I'm sick of it. [*Aside*
  True. How well she plays the harpsichord and harp !
How well she sings to them ! Who'er would prove
The power of song, should hear thy neighbour sing,
Especially a love song !
  Wild. Does she sing
Such songs to thee ?
  True. Oh, yes, and constantly !
For such I ever ask her.

Wild. Forward minx !   [*Aside*
Maids should not sing love songs to gentlemen !
Think'st neighbour Constance is a girl to love ?
  True. A girl to love ?—Ay, and with all her soul !
  Wild. How know you that ?
  True. I have studied close the sex.
  Wild. You town-rakes are the devil for the sex ! [*Aside*
  True. Not your most sensitive and serious maid
I'd always take for deep impressions. " Mind
" The adage of the bow. The pensive brow
" I 've oft seen bright in wedlock, and anon
" O'ercast in widowhood ; then bright again,
" Ere half the season of the weeds was out.
" While, in the airy one, I've known one cloud
" Forerunner of a gloom that ne'er cleared up—
" So it would prove with neighbour Constance. Not
" On superficial ground she'll ever love ;
' But once she does, the odds are ten to one,"
Her first love is her last !
  Wild. I wish I ne'er
Had come to town ! I was a happy man
Among my dogs and horses. [*Aside.* Hast thou broke
Thy passion to her ?
  True. Never.
  Wild. Never ?
  True. No.
I hoped you'd act my proxy there.
  Wild. I thank you.
  True. I knew 'twould be a pleasure to you.
  Wild. Yes ;
A pleasure !—an unutterable pleasure !
  True. Thank you ! You make my happiness your own
                               [*Crosses,* L.
  Wild. I do.
  True. I see you do. Dear Master Wildrake !
Oh, what a blessing is a friend in need,
You'll go and court your neighbour for me ?
  Wild. Yes.
  True. And says she "nay" at first, you'll press again ?
  Wild. Ay, and again !
  True. There's one thing I mistrust—yea, most mistrust,
That of my poor deserts you'll make too much.

Wild. Fear anything but that.

True. 'Twere better far,
You slightly spoke of them.

Wild. You think so?

True. Yes,
Or rather did not speak of them at all.

Wild. You think so?

True. Yes.*

Wild. Then I'll not say a word
About them.

True. Thank you! "A judicious friend
" Is better than a zealous.—You are both!
" I see you'll plead my cause as 'twere your own ;
" Then stay in town and win your neighbour for me,
" Make me the envy of a score of men
" That die for her as I do."—Make her mine,
And when the last " Amen!" declares complete
The mystic tying of the holy knot,
And 'fore the priest a blushing wife she stands,
Be thine the right to claim the second kiss
She pays for change from maidenhood to wifehood.

[*Goes out,* L.

Wild. Take that thyself! The first be mine, or none '
A man in love with neighbour Constance !—Never
Dreamed I that such a thing could come to pass !
Such person, such endowments, such a soul !
I never thought to ask myself before
If she were man or woman ! Suitors, too,
Dying for her ! I'll e'en make one among 'em !
Woo her to go to church along with him,
And for my pains, the privilege to take
The second kiss? I'll take the second kiss,
And first one, too—and last ! No man shall touch
Her lips but me. I'll massacre the man
That looks upon her ! Yet what chance have I
With lovers of the town, whose study 'tis
To please your lady belles !—who dress, walk, talk,
To hit their tastes—what chance, a country squire
Like me ? Yet your true fair, I 've heard, prefers
The man before his coat at any time,
And such a one must neighbour Constance be.
I'll show a limb with any of them ! Silks

I'll wear, nor keep my legs in cases more.
I'll learn to dance town-dances, and frequent
Their concerts ! Die away at melting strains
Or seem to do so—far the easier thing,
And as effective, quite ; leave naught undone
To conquer neighbour Constance.

Enter LASH, L.

Lash. Sir.
Wild. Well, sir.
Lash. So please you, sir, your horse is at the door.
Wild. Unsaddle him again, and put him up.
And, hark you, get a tailor for me, sir—
The rarest can be found.
Lash. The man's below, sir,
That owns the mare your worship thought to buy
Wild. Tell him I do not want her, sir.
Lash. I vow,
You will not find her like in Lincolnshire
Wild. Go to ! She's spavined.
Lash. Sir !
Wild. Touched in the wind.
Lash. I trust my master be not touched in the head !
I vow, a faultless beast !   [*Aside.*
Wild. I want her not,
And that's your answer—Go to the hosier's, sir,
And bid him send me samples of his gear,
Of twenty different kinds.
Lash. I will, sir.—Sir !
Wild. Well, sir.
Lash. Squire Brush's huntsman's here, and says
His master's kennel is for sale.
Wild. The dogs
Are only fit for hanging !
Lash. Finer bred—
Wild. Sirrah, if more to me thou talk'st of dogs,
Horses, or aught that to thy craft belongs,
Thou may'st go hang for me !—A cordwainer
Go fetch me straight—the choicest in the town.
Away, sir ! Do thy errands smart and well,
As thou canst crack thy whip !—[*Exit Lash, L.*]—Dear
      neighbour Constance,
'll give up horses, dogs, and all, for thee !   [*Exit,* R.

SCENE II.—*Toilette-table, Sofa, &c., discovered.*

Enter WIDOW GREEN *and* LYDIA, R.

Widow G. Lydia, my gloves. If Master Waller calls,
I shall be in at three; and say the same
To old Sir William Fondlove. Tarry yet!—
What progress, think you, make I in the heart
Of fair young Master Waller? Gods, my girl,
It is a heart to win and man as well!
How speed I, think you? Didst, as I desired,
Detain him in my absence when he called,
And, without seeming, sound him touching me?
    Lydia. (L. C.) Yes.
    Widow G. And affects he me, or not? How guess
        you?   .
What said he of me? Looked he balked, or not,
To find me not at home? Inquired he, when
I would be back, as much he longed to see me?
What did he—said he? Come!—Is he in love,
Or like to fall into it? Goes well my game,
Or shall I have my labour for my pains?
    Lydia. I think he is in love.—Oh, poor evasion!
Oh, to love truth, and yet not dare to speak it!   [*Aside.*
    Widow G. You think he is in love. I'm sure of it,
As well have asked you has he eyes and ears,
And brain and heart to use them? Maids do throw
Trick after trick away, but widows know
To play their cards! How am I looking, Lydia?
    Lydia. E'en as you ever look.
    Widow G. Handsome, my girl?
Eh? Clear in my complexion? Eh?—brimful
Of spirits? not too much of me, nor yet
Too little?—Eh?—A woman worth a man?
" Look at me, Lydia! Would you credit, girl,
" I was a scare-crow before marriage?
    " *Lydia.* Nay!—
    Widow G. "Girl, but I tell thee, 'yea.' That gown
        of thine—
" And thou art slender—would have hung about me!
" There's something of me now! good sooth, enough!"
Lydia, I'm quite contented with myself;
I'm just the thing, methinks, a widow should be.

So Master Waller, you believe, affects me !
But, Lydia, not enough to hook the fish ;
To prove the angler's skill, it must be caught ;
And lovers, Lydia, like the angler's prey—
Which, when he draws it near the landing place,
Takes warning, and runs out the slender line,
And with a spring perchance jerks off the hold—
When we do fish for them, aud hook, and think
They are all but in the creel, will make the dart
That sets them free to roam the flood again !
    Lydia. Is't so ?
    Widow G. Thou'lt find it so, or better luck
Than many another maid ! Now mark me, Lydia ;
Sir William Fondlove fancies me. 'Tis well !
I do not fancy him ! What should I do
With an old man ?—Attend upon the gout,
Or the rheumatics ! Wrap me in the cloud
Of a darkened chamber—'stead of shining out,
The sun of balls, and routs, and gala days !
But he affects me, Lydia ; so he may !
Now take a lesson from me—Jealousy
Had better go with open, naked breast,
Than pin or button with a gem—Less plague,
The plague spot : that doth speedy make an end
One way or t'other, girl—Yet never love
Was warm without a spice of jealousy.
Thy lesson now—Sir William Fondlove's rich,
And riches, though they're paste, yet, being many,
The jewel love we often cast away for.
I use him but for Master Waller's sake.
Dost like my policy ?
    Lydia. You will not chide me ?
    Widow G. Nay, Lydia, I do like to hear thy thoughts
They are such novel things—plants that do thrive
With country air ! I marvel still they flower,
And thou so long in town ! Speak freely, girl !
    Lydia. I cannot think love thrives by artifice,
Or can disguise its mood, aud show its face.
I would not hide one portion of my heart,
Where I did give it, and did feel 'twas right,
Nor feign a wish, to mask a wish that was,
Howe'er to keep it. For no cause except

Myself would I be loved. What wer't tc me
My lover valued me the more, the more
He saw me comely in another's eyes,
When his alone the vision I would show
Becoming to ?   I have sought the reason oft,
They paint Love as a child, and still have thought,
It was because true love, like infancy,
Frank, trusting, unobservant of its mood,
Doth show its wish at once, and means no more!

    Widow G. Thou'lt find out better when thy time dotr
       come.
Now would'st believe I love not Master Waller ?
I never knew what love was, Lydia ;
That is, as your romancers have it.   First,
I married for a fortune.   Having that,
And being freed from him that brought it me,
I marry now, to please my vanity,
A man that is the fashion.   Oh, the delight
Of a sensation, and yourself the cause !
To note the stir of eyes, and ears, and tongues,
When they do usher Mistress Waller in,
Late Widow Green, her hand upon the arm
Of her young handsome husband !   How my fan
Will be in requisition—I do feel
My heart begin to flutter now—my blood
To mount into my cheek !   My honey-moon
Will be a month of triumphs !—" Mistress Waller !"
That name, for which a score of damsels sigh,
And but the widow had the wit to win !
Why, it will be the talk of East and West,
And North and South !—The children loved the man
And lost him so—I liked, but there I stopped ;
For what is it to love, but mind, and heart,
And soul upon another to depend ?
Depend upon another !—Nothing be
But what another wills !   Give up the rights
Of mine own brain and heart !—I thank my stars
I never came to that extremity !   [*Exit,* L.

    Lydia. She never loved, indeed !—She knows not love,
Except what's told of it !—She never felt it.
To stem a torrent, easy, looking at it ;
But once you venture in, you nothing know

Except the speed with which you're borne away,
Howe'er you strive to check it.   She suspects not
Her maid, not she, brings Master Waller hither.
Nor dare I undeceive her   Well might she say
Her young and handsome husband !   Yet his face
And person are the least of him, and vanish
When shines his soul out through his open eye !
He all but says he loves me !—His respect
Has vanquished me !   He looks the will to speak
His passion, and the fear that ties his tongue—
The fear ?—He loves not honestly !—and yet
I'll swear he loves !—I'll swear he honours me !
It is but my condition is a bar,
Denies him give me all.   But knew he me,
As I do know myself !—Whate'er his purpose,
When next we speak, he shall declare it to me.   [*Exit*, R.

SCENE III.—*Sir William Fondlove's.*

Enter CONSTANCE, *dressed for riding, and* PHŒBE, R.

Con. Well, Phœbe, would you know me ?   Are those
      locks
That cluster on my forehead and my cheek,
Sufficient mask ?   Show I what I would seem,
A lady for the chase ?   My darkened brows
And heightened colour, foreign to my face,
Do they my face pass off for stranger, too ?
What think you ?
      Phœbe. That he'll ne'er discover you.
      Con. Then send him to me—say a lady wants
To speak with him—unless indeed it be
A man in lady's gear—I look so bold,
And speak so gruff !—Away ! [*Exit Phœbe*, R.] That
      am glad
He stays in town, I own ; but if I am,
'Tis only for the tricks I'll play upon him ;
And now begin—persuading him his fame
Hath made me fancy him, and brought me hither
On visit to his worship.   Soft ! his foot !
This he ?—Why, what has metamorphosed him,
And changed my sportsman to fine gentleman ?
Well he becomes his clothes !—But I must check my won-
      der,

Lest I forget myself—Why, what an air
The fellow hath!—A man to set a cap at!

Enter WILDRAKE, R.

Wild. Kind lady, I attend your fair commands.
Con. "My veiléd face denies me justice, sir,
" Else would you see a maiden's blushing cheek
" Do penance for her forwardness, too late,
" I own, repented of.   Yet, if 'tis true,
" By our own hearts of others we may judge,
" Mine in no peril lies, that's shown to you,
" Whose heart, I'm sure, is noble."   Worthy sir,
Souls attract souls, when they're of kindred vein.
The life that you love, I love.   Well I know,
'Mongst those who breast the feats of the bold chase
You stand without a peer; and for myself,
I dare avow, 'mong such none follows them
With heartier glee than I do.
        Wild. Churl were he
That would gainsay you, madam!
        Con. [*Courtesying.*] What delight
To back the flying steed, that challenges
The wind for speed!—seems native more of air
Than earth!—whose burden only lends him fire!
Whose soul, in his task, turns labour into sport!
Who makes your pastime his!   I sit him now!
He takes away my breath!—He makes me reel
I touch not earth—I see not—hear not—All
Is ecstacy of motion!
        Wild. You are used,
I see, to the chase.
        Con. I am, Sir!   Then the leap!
To see the saucy barrier, and know
The mettle that can clear it.   Then your time
To prove you master of the manage.   Now
You keep him well together for a space,
Both horse and rider braced as you were one,
Scanning the distance—then you give him rein,
And let him fly at it, and o'er he goes,
Light as a bird on wing.
        Wild. Twere a bold leap,
I see, that turned you, madam

Con. [*Courtesying.*] Sir, you're good!
And then the hounds, sir! Nothing I admire
Beyond the running of the well-trained pack.
The training's everything! Keen on the scent!
At fault none losing heart!—but all at work!
None leaving his task to another!—answering
The watchful huntsman's caution, check, or cheer,
As steed his rider's rein! Away they go!
How close they keep together!—What a pack!
Nor turn, nor ditch, nor stream divides them—as
They moved with one intelligence, act, will!
And then the concert they keep up!—enough
To make one tenant of the merry wood,
To list their jocund music!
 Wild. You describe
The huntsman's pastime to the life!
 Con. I love it!
To wood and glen, hamlet and town, it is
A laughing holiday!—Not a hill-top
But's then alive!—Footmen with horsemen vie,
All earth's astir, roused with the revelry
Of vigor, health, and joy! Cheer awakes cheer,
While Echo's mimic tongue, that never tires,
Keeps up the hearty din! Each face is then
Its neighbour's glass—where gladness sees itself
And, at the bright reflection, grows more glad!
Breaks into tenfold mirth!—laughs like a child!
Would make a gift of its heart, it is so free!
Would scarce accept a kingdom, 'tis so rich!
Shakes hands with all, and vows it never knew
That life was life before!   [*Crosses,* L.
 Wild. Nay, every way
You do fair justice, lady, to the chase;
But fancies change.
 Con. Such fancy is not mine.
 Wild. I would it were not mine, for your fair sake.
I have quite given o'er the chase.
 Con. You say not so!
 Wild. Forsworn, indeed, the sportsman's life, and
  grown,
As you may partly see, town gentleman.
I care not now to mount a steed, unless

To amble 'long the street ; no paces mind,
Except my own, to walk the drawing-room,
Or in the ball-room to come off with grace :
No leap for me, to match the light coupé ;
No music like the violin and harp,
To which the huntsman's dog and horn, I find,
Are somewhat coarse and homely minstrelsy :
Then fields of ill-dressed rustics, you'll confess,
Are well exchanged for rooms of beaux and belles ;
In short, I've ta'en another thought of life—
Become another man !

  Con. The cause, I pray ?
  Wild. The cause of causes, lady.
  Con. He's in love.   [*Aside.*
  Wild. To you, of women, I would name it last ;
Yet your frank bearing merits like return :
I that did hunt the game, am caught myself,
In chase I never dreamed of !   [*Exit,* R.
  Con. He is in love !
Wildrake's in love ! 'Tis that keeps him in town,
Turns him from sportsman to town-gentleman.
I never dreamed that he could be in love !
In love with whom ?—I'll find the vixen out !
What right has she to set her cap at him ?
I warrant me, a forward artful minx !
I hate him worse than ever.—I'll do all
I can to spoil the match. He'll never marry—
Sure he will never marry ! He will have
More sense than that ! " My back doth ope and shut-
" My temples throb and shoot—I 'm cold and hot !"
Were he to marry, there would be an end
To neighbour Constance—neighbour Wildrake—why
I should not know myself !

    Enter TRUEWORTH, L.

Dear Master Trueworth,
What think you ?—Neighbour Wildrake is in love !
In love !—would you believe it, Master Trueworth ?
Ne'er heed my dress and looks, but answer me.
Know'st thou of any lady he has seen,
That's like to cozen him ?
  True. I am not sure—
We talked to-day about the Widow **Green** !

Con. Her that my father fancies.—Let him wed her!
Marry her to-morrow—if he will, to-night.
I can't spare neighbour Wildrake—neighbour Wildrake!
Although I would not marry him myself,
I could not bear that other married him!
Go to my father—[*Crosses*, R.] 'tis a proper match!
He has my leave! He's welcome to bring home
The Widow Green. I'll give up house and all!
She would be mad to marry neighbour Wildrake:
He would wear out her patience—plague her to death,
As he does me.—She must not marry him!

    [*Exeunt Trueworth* C., *Constance*, R

    END OF ACT II.

    •

    ACT III.

  SCENE I.—*A Room at Widow Green's.*

  Enter LYDIA, R., MASTER WALLER *following*

Wal. But thou shalt hear me, gentle Lydia.
Sweet maiden, thou art frightened at thyself!
Thy own perfections 'tis that talk to thee.
Thy beauty rich!—thy richer grace!—thy mind,
More rich again than that, though richest each!
Except for these, I had no tongue for thee,
Eyes for thee!—ears!—had never followed thee!—
Had never loved thee, Lydia!—Hear me!—
 Lydia. Love
Should seek its match.—No match am I for thee.
 Wal. Right! Love should seek its match; and that is,
  love
Or nothing! Station—fortune—find their match
In things resembling them. They are not love!
Comes love (that subtle essence, without which
Life were but leaden dullness!—weariness!
A plodding trudger on a heavy road!)
Comes it of title-deeds, which fools may boast?
Or coffers, vilest hands may hold the keys of?
Or that ethereal lamp that lights the eyes

To shed their sparkling lustre o'er the face,
Gives to the velvet skin its blushing glow,
And burns as bright beneath the peasant's roof,
As roof of palaced prince? Yes! Love should seek
Its match—then give my love its match in thine,
Its match, which in thy gentle breast doth lodge
So rich—so earthly, heavenly fair and rich,
As monarchs have no thought of on their thrones,
Which kingdoms do bear up.
 Lydia. Wast thou a monarch,
Me wouldst thou make thy queen?
  Wal. I would!
  Lydia. What!—Pass
A princess by for me!
  Wal. I would.
  Lydia. Suppose
Thy subjects would prevent thee?
  Wal. Then, in spite
Of them!
  Lydia. Suppose they were too strong for thee?
  Wal. Why, then I'd give them up my throne—content
With that thou'dst yield me in thy gentle breast.
  Lydia. Can subjects do what monarchs do?
  Wal. Far more!
Far less!
  Lydia. Among those things, were more their power
Is marriage one?
  Wal. Yes.
  Lydia. And no part of love,
You say, is rank or wealth?
  Wal. No part of love.
  Lydia. Is marriage part of love?
  Wal. At times it is,
At times is not. Men love and marry—love
And marry not.
  Lydia. Then have they not the power;
So must they hapless part with those they love.
  Wal. Oh, no! not part! How could they love and
  part?
  Lydia. How could they love, not part, not free to wed!
  Wal. Alone in marriage doth not union lie!
  Lydia. Alone where hands are free!—Oh, yes—alone!

Love that is ove, bestoweth all it can!
It is protection, if 'tis anything;
Which nothing in its object leaves exposed
Its care can shelter.—Love that's free to wed,
Not wedding, doth profane the name of love,
Which is, on high authority to Earth's,
(For Heaven did sit approving at its feast,)
A holy thing!—Why make you love to me?
Women whose hearts are free, by nature tender,
Theft fancies hit by those they are besought by,
Do first impressions quickly—deeply take;
And, balked in their election, have been known
To droop a whole life through! Gain for a maid
A broken heart!—to barter her young love,
And find she changed it for a counterfeit!   [*Crosses, R*

Wal. If there is truth in man, I love thee!—Hear me
In wedlock, families claim property,—
Old notions, which we needs must humour often,
Bar us to wed where we are forced to love!
Thou hear'st?
     Lydia. I do.
     Wal. My family is proud;
Our ancestor whose arms we bear, did win
An earldom by his deeds. 'Tis not enough
I please myself!—I must please others, who
Desert in wealth and station only see.
Thou hear'st?
     Lydia. I do.
     Wal. I cannot marry thee,—
And must I lose thee?—Do not turn away!
Without the altar I can honour thee!
Can cherish thee, nor swear it to the priest
For more than life I love thee!
     Lydia. Say thou hat'st me,
And I'll believe thee.—Wherein differs love
From hate, to do the work of hate—destroy?
Thy ancestor won title by his deeds!
Was one of them to teach an honest maid
The deed of sin—first steal her love, and then
Her virtue? If thy family is proud,
Mine. Sir, is worthy! If we are poor, the lack
Of riches, Sir, is not the lack of shame!

That I should act a part, would raise a blush,
Nor fear to burn an honest brother's cheek!
Thou wouldst share a throne with me!—Thou wouldst
    rob me of
A throne!—reduce me from dominion to
Base vassalage!   Pull off my crown for me,
And give my forehead in its place a brand!
You have insulted me.—To show you, Sir,
The heart you make so light of—you are beloved—
But she that tells you so, tells you beside
She ne'er beholds you more!   [*Exit,* R

   Wal. Stay, Lydia!—No!—
'Tis vain!   She is in virtue resolute,
As she is bland and tender in affection.
She is a miracle, beholding which,
Wonder doth grow on wonder!—" What a maid!
" No mood but doth become her—yea, adorn her.
" She turns unsightly anger into beauty!
" Sour scorn grows sweetness, touching her sweet lips!
" And indignation, lighting on her brow,
" Transforms to brightness, as the cloud to gold
" That overhangs the sun!   I love her!—Ay!
" And all the throes of serious passion feel,
" At thought of losing her!"—So my light love,
Which but her person did at first affect,
Her soul has metamorphosed—made a thing
Of solid thoughts and wishes—I must have her!

Enter WIDOW GREEN, L., *unnoticed by Waller, who conti*
    nues abstracted, R.

   Widow G. (L. C.) What!—Master Waller, and contem
    plative!
Presumptive proof of love!   Of me he thinks!   .
Revolves the point, " to be or not to be!"
" To be!" by all the triumphs of my sex!
There was a sigh!   My life upon't, that sigh,
If construed, would translate " Dear Widow Green!"
   Wal. Enchanting woman!   [*Takes the stage, musing.*
   Widow G. That is I!—most deep
Abstraction, sure concomitant of love.
Now could I see his busy fancy's painting,
How should I blush to gaze upon myself

Wal. The matchless form of woman! The choice culling
Of the aspiring artist, whose ambition
Robs Nature to out-do her—the perfections
Of her rare various workmanship combines
To aggrandize his art at Nature's cost,
And makes a paragon!   `Crosses*, R.
   Widow G. (L. C.) Gods! how he draws me!
Soon as he sees me, at my feet he falls!
Good Master Waller! (C.)
   Wal. (R. C.) Ha! The Widow Green!
   Widow G. He is confounded!—So am I. Oh, dear!
How catching is emotion.—He can't speak!
Oh, beautiful confusion! Amiable
Excess of modesty, with passion struggling!
Now comes he to declare himself, but wants .
The courage.—I will help him.—Master Waller!

      Enter SIR WILLIAM FONDLOVE, L.

   Sir W. Dear Widow Green!
   Widow G. (C.) Sir William Fondlove!
   Wal. Thank
My lucky stars!   [*Aside*, R., *and retires up a little.*
   Widow G. I would he had the gout,
And kept his room! [*Aside.*]—you're welcome, dear Sir
    William!
'Tis very, very kind of you to call.
Sir William Fondlove—Master Waller. [*They advance a
    little.*] Pray
Be seated, gentlemen. He shall requite me
For his untimely visit. Though the nail
Be driven home, it may the clinching lack
To make the hold complete! For that I'll use him.
    [*Aside—With ceremony they take chairs and sit. Wal-
    ler gets gradually away from the Widow to the* R.
You are looking monstrous well, Sir William! and
No wonder. You're a mine of happy spirits!
Some women talk of such and such a style
Of features in a man.—Give me good humour;
That lights the homeliest visage up with beauty,
And makes the face where beauty is already,
Quite irresistible!*

   * The sides in this scene may be reversed, if it would improve the business

Sir W. That's hitting hard.   [*Aside.*
Dear Widow Green, don't say so ! On my life,
You flatter me.—You almost make me blush.
     Widow G. I durst not turn to Master Waller now,
Nor need I.—I can fancy how he looks !
1 warrant me he scowls on poor Sir William,
As he could eat him up.—I will improve
His discontent, and so make sure of him.   [*Aside.*
I flatter you, Sir William ? Oh, you men !
You men, that talk so meek, and all the while
Do know so well your power ! Who would think
You had a marriageable daughter ! You
Did marry very young.
     Sir W. A boy !—A boy,
Who knew not his own mind.
     Widow G. Your daughter's twenty.
Come, you at least were twenty when you married
That makes you forty.
     Sir W. Oh, dear !—Widow Green.
     Widow G. Not forty ?
     Sir W. You do quite embarrass me !
1 own I have the feelings of a boy,
The freshness and the glow of springtime yet,
The relish yet for my young school-day's sports ;
Could whip a top—could shoot a taw—could play
At prison-bars and leap-frog, so I might—
Not with a limb, perhaps, as supple, but
With quite as supple will.—Yet I confess
To more than forty !
     Widow G. Do you say so ? Well,
I'll never guess a man's age by his looks
Again.—Poor Master Waller ! He must writhe
To hear I think Sir William is so young.
I'll turn his visit yet to more account.   [*Aside.*
A handsome ring, Sir William, that you wear !
     Sir W. Pray look at it.
     Widow G. The mention of a ring
Will take away his breath.   [*Aside.*
     Wal. She must be mine,
Whate'er her terms !   [*Aside.*
     Widow G. I'll steal a look at him !
     Wal What ! though it be the ring ? the marriage ring !

If that she sticks at, she deserves to wear it !
Oh, the debate which love and prudence hold !   [*Aside.*
  Widow G. How highly he is wrought upon !—His
    hands
Are clenched !—I warrant me his frame doth shake !
Poor Master Waller !   I have filled his heart
Brimful with passion for me.—The delight
Of proving thus my power !
  Sir W. Dear Widow Green !
She hears not !   How the ring hath set her thinking !
I'll try and make her jealous. [*Aside.*]—Widow Green !
  Widow G. Sir William Fondlove !
  Sir W. Would you think that ring
Could tell a story ?
  Widow G. Could it ?   Ah, Sir William !
I fear you are a rogue.
  Sir W. Oh, no !
  Widow G. You are !
  Sir W. No, on my honour !   Would you like to hear
The story of the ring ?
  Widow G. Much,—very much.
  Sir W. Think'st we may venture draw our chairs apart
A little more from Master Waller ?
  Widow G. Yes.
He'll bring it to a scene !   Dear—dear Sir William,
How much I am obliged to him !   A scene !
Gods, we shall have a scene !—Good Master Waller,
Your leave, I pray you, for a minute, while
Sir William says a word or two to me.
He durst not trust his tongue for jealousy.   [*Aside*
Now, dear Sir William.
  Sir W. You must promise me
You will not think me vain.
  Widow G. No fear of that.
  Sir W. Nor given to boast.
  Widow. Oh ! dear Sir William !
  Sir W. Nor
A flirt !
  Widow G. Oh ! who would take you for a flirt ?
  Sir W. How very kind you are !
  Widow G. Go on, Sir William.
  Sir W. Upon my life, I fear you'll think me vain !

I'm covered with confusion at the thought
Of what I've done.   'Twas very, very wrong
To promise you the story of the ring;
Men should not talk of such things.
 Widow G. Such as what ?
As ladies' favours ?
 Sir W. 'Pon my life, I feel
As I were like to sink into the earth.
 Widow G. A lady, then, it was gave you the ring ?
 Sir W. Don't ask me to say yes, but only scan
The inside of the ring.   How much she's moved ! [*Aside*
 Wal. (R. C.) [*Aside.*] They to each other company
  enough!
I, company for no one but myself.
I'll take my leave, nor trouble them to pay
The compliments of parting.   Lydia! Lydia! [*Exit,* R.
 Widow G. What's here ?   " Eliza !"—So, it was a la-
  dy !
How wondrously does Master Waller bear it !
He surely will not hold much longer out.   [*Aside*
Sir William ! Nay, look up !   What cause to cast
Your eyes upon the ground ?   What an' it were
A lady ?
 Sir W. You're not angry ?
 Widow G. No !
 Sir W. She is.
I'll take the tone she speaks in 'gainst the word,
For fifty crowns. [*Aside.*]—I have not told you all
About the ring; though I would sooner die
Than play the braggart!—yet, as truth is truth,
And, told by halves, may from a simple thing,
By misconstruction, to a monster grow,
I'll tell the whole truth !
 Widow G. Dear Sir William, do !
 Sir W. The lady was a maid, and very young ;
Nor there in justice to her must I stop,
But say that she was beautiful as young,
And add to that that she was learned, too,
" Almost enough to win for her that title,
" Our sex, in poor conceit of their own merits
" And narrow spirit of monopoly,
" And jealousy which gallantry eschews,

" Do give to women who assert their right
" To minds as well as we.
  " *Widow G.* What! a blue stocking?
  Sir W. " I see.—She'll come to calling names at last.
                          " [*Aside.*

" I should offend myself to quote the term.
" But to return, for yet I have not done ;
" And further yet may go, then progress on"
That she was young, that she was beautiful,
A wit and learned are naught to what's to come—
She had a heart !—
  Widow G. [*who, during Sir William's speech has turned*
    gradually.] What, Master Waller gone ! [*Aside.*
  Sir W. I say she had a heart—
  Widow G. [*Starting up,* c.—*Sir William also.*] A plague
    upon her !
  Sir W. (L. C.) I knew she would break out ! [*Aside*
  Widow G. Here, take the ring.
It has ruined me !
  Sir W. I vow thou hast no cause
For anger !
  Widow G. Have I not ? I am undone,
And all about that bauble of a ring. ˙
  Sir W. You're right, it is a bauble.
  Widow G. And the minx
That gave it thee !
  Sir W. You're right, she was a minx.
  knew she'd come to calling names at last.   [*Aside.*
  Widow G. Sir William Fondlove, leave me.
  Sir W. Widow Green !—
  Widow G. You have undone me, Sir !
  Sir W. Don't say so !—Don't !
It was a girl—a child gave me the ring !
  Widow G. Do you hear me, Sir ! I bade you leave me
  " *Sir W.* If
" I thought you were so jealous.
  " *Widow G.* Jealous, Sir !
" Sir William ! quit my house.
  " *Sir W.* A little girl
' To make you jealous !
  " *Widow G.* Sir, you'll drive me mad !
  " *Sir W.* A child, a perfect child, not ten years old !

" *Widow G.* Sir, I would be alone, sir !

" *Sir W.* Young enough
" To dandle still her doll !

" *Widow G.* Sir William Fondlove !—

" *Sir W.* Dear Widow Green !

" *Widow G.*" I hate you, sir !—Detest you !—Never
    wish
To see you more ! You have ruined me !—Undone me !
A blighted life I wear, and all through you !
The fairest hopes that ever woman nourished
You've cankered in the very blowing ! bloom,
And sweet destroyed, and nothing left me, but
The melancholy stem.

    Sir W. And all about
A little slut I gave a rattle to !—
Would pester me for gingerbread and comfits !
A little roguish feigning !—A love trick
I played to prove your love !

    Widow G. Sir William Fondlove !
If of my own house you'll not suffer me
To be the mistress, I will leave it to you !

    Sir W. Dear Widow Green ! The ring—

    Widow G. Confound the ring,
The donor of it, thee, and everything !

                 [*Exit*, R. 1 E. *hurriedly.*

    Sir W. She is over head and ears in love with me.
She's mad with love ! There's love and all its signs .
She's jealous of me unto very death !
Poor Widow Green ! I warrant she is now
In tears !—I think I hear her sob !—Poor thing !
Sir William ! oh, Sir William ! you have raised
A furious tempest ! Set your wits to work
To turn it to a calm. No question that
She loves me !—None, then, that she'll take me ! So
I'll have the marriage settlements made out
To-morrow, and a special licence got,
And marry her the next day ! I will make
Quick work of it, and take her by surprise !
Who but a widower a widow's match ;
What could she see with else but partial eyes
To guess me only forty ! I'm a wonder !
What shall I pass for in my wedding suit !

I vow, I am a puzzle to myself,
As well as all the world besides.—Odds life!
To win the heart of buxom Widow Green!   [*Exit,* L.

WIDOW GREEN *re-enters with* LYDIA, R. 1 E.

Widow G. At last the dotard's gone! Fly, Lydia, fly
This letter bear to Master Waller straight;
Quick, quick, or I'm undone!—He is abused.
And I must undeceive him—own my love,
And heart and hand at his disposal lay.
Answer me not, my girl—Obey me!—Fly.   [*Exit,* R

Lydia. Untowardly it falls!—I had resolved
This hour to tell her I must quit her service!
Go to his house!—I will not disobey
Her last commands!—I'll leave it at the door,
And as it closes on me, think I take
One more adieu of him!—Hard destiny!   [*Exit,* L

SCENE II.—*A Room in Sir William Fondlove's*

Enter CONSTANCE, R.

Con. The booby! He must fall in love, indeed!
And now he's naught but sentimental looks
And sentences pronounced 'twixt breath and voice!
And attitudes of tender languishment!
Nor can I get from him the name of her
Hath turned him from a stock into a fool.
He hems and haws, now titters, now looks grave!
Begins to speak and halts!—takes off his eyes
To fall in contemplation on a chair,
A table, or the ceiling, wall, or floor!
I'll plague him worse and worse! Oh, here he comes!

Enter WILDRAKE, L.

Wild. Despite her spiteful usage, I'm resolved
To tell her now. Dear neighbour Constance!
Con. Fool!
Accost me like a lady, Sir! I hate
The name of neighbour!
Wild. Mistress Constance, then—
I'll call thee that.
Con. Don't call me anything!

I hate to hear thee speak—to look at thee,
To dwell in the same house with thee!

Wild. In what
Have I offended ?

Con. What!—I hate an ape!

Wild. An ape!

Con. Who bade thee ape the gentleman ?
And put on dress that don't belong to thee ?
Go! change thee with thy whipper-in or huntsman,
And none will doubt thou wearest thy own clothes.

Wild. A pretty pass! Mocked for the very dress
I bought to pleasure her! Untoward things
Are women! [*Aside—walks backwards and forwards.*

Con. Do you call that walking ? Pray,
What makes you twist your body so, and take
Such pains to turn your toes out ? If you'd walk,
Walk thus! walk like a man, as I do now! [*Walking.*
Is yours the way a gentleman should walk ?
You neither walk like man nor gentleman !
I'll show you how you walk. [*Mimicks him.*] Do you call
          that walking ?

Wild. My thanks for a drill-sergeant twice a day
For her sake ! [*Aside.*

Con. Now, of all things in the world,
What made you dance last night ?

Wild. What made me dance ?

Con. Right! It was anything but dancing! Steps
That never came from dancing school—nor English,
Nor Scotch, nor Irish!—You must try to cut,
And how you did it! [*Cuts.*] That's the way to cut!
And then you chassè! Thus you went, and thus,
          [*Mimicking him.*
As though you had been playing at hop, step,
And jump!—And yet you looked so monstrous pleased,
And played the simpleton with such a grace,
Taking the tittering for compliment !
I could have boxed you soundly for't. Ten times,
Denied I that I knew you.

Wild. Twenty guineas
Were better in the gutter thrown, than gone
To fee a dancing master ! [*Aside.*

Con. And you're grown

An amateur in music!—What fine air
Was that you praised last night?—" The Widow Jones !"
A country jig they've turned into a song.
You asked " if it had come from Italy ?"
The lady blushed, and held her peace, and then
You blushed and said, " Perhaps it came from France !
And then when blushed the lady more, nor spoke,
You said, " At least it came from Germany !"
The air was English !—a true English air ;
A downright English air ! A common air,
Old as " When Good King Arthur." Not a square,
Court, alley, street, or lane about the town,
In which it is not whistled, played, or sung !
But you must have it come from Italy,
Or Germany, or France.—Go home ! Go home !
To Lincolnshire, and mind thy dog and horn !
You'll never do for town ! " The Widow Jones"
To come from Italy ! Stay not in town,
Or you'll be married to the Widow Jones,
Since you've forsworn, you say, the Widow Green !
And morn and night they'll din your ears with her !
" Well met, dear Master Wildrake.—A fine day !
Pray, can you tell whence came the Widow Jones ?"
They love a jest in town !—To Lincolnshire !
You'll never do for town !—To Lincolnshire !
" The Widow Jones" to come from Italy !   [*Exit,* &c.
   Wild. Confound the Widow Jones ! 'Tis true ! The
    air,
Well as the huntsman's triple 'most I know,
But knew not then, indeed, 'twas so disguised
With shakes and flourishes, outlandish things,
That mar, not grace, an honest English song !
Howe'er, the mischief's done ! and as for her,
She is either into hate or madness fallen.
If madness, would she had her wits again,
Or I my heart—If hate—my love's undone ;
I'll give her up. I'll e'en to Master Trueworth,
Confess my treason—own my punishment—
Take horse, and back again to Lincolnshire !   [*Exit,* L.
   " *Con.* [*Returning.*] Not here ! I trust I have not gone
    too far ! ·
" If he should quit the house ! Go out of town !

" Poor neighbour Wildrake !   Little does he owe me !
" From childhood I've been used to plague him thus.
" Why would he fall in love, and spoil it all !
" I feel as I could cry !   He has no right
" To marry any one ?   What wants he with
" A wife ?   Has he not plague enough in me ?
" Would he be plagued with anybody else ?
" Ever since I have lived in town I 've felt
" The want of neighbour Wildrake !   Not a soul
" Besides I care to quarrel with ; and now
" He goes and gives himself to another !—What !
" Am I in love with neighbour Wildrake ?—No.
" I only would not have him marry—marry !
" Sooner I'd have him dead than have him marry !

[Exit, r.

END OF ACT III.

ACT IV.

Scene I.—*A Room in Master Waller's House.*

Enter Alice hastily, l.

Alice. [*Speaking to the outside.*] Fly, Stephen, to the
     door ! your rapier ! quick !—
Our master is beset, because of one
Whose part he takes, a maid, whom lawless men
Would lawlessly entreat !   In what a world
We live !—How do I shake !—With what address
[Looking out of window
He lays about him, and his other arm
Engaged, in charge of her whom he defends !
A damsel worth a broil !—Now, Stephen, now !
Take off the odds, brave lad, and turn the scale !
" I would I were a swordsman !   How he makes
" His rapier fly !—Well done !—Oh, Heaven, there's blood,
" But on the side that's wrong !—Well done, good Ste-
     phen !
" Pray Heaven no life be ta'en !—Lay on, brave lad !
" He has marked his man again !   Good lad—Well done !
" I pray no mischief come !—Press on him, Stephen !

" Now gives he ground—Follow thy advantage up!
" Allow no pause for breath !—Hit him again !
" Forbid it end in death !—Lounge home, good Stephen!
" How fast he now retreats ! That spring, I'll swear,
' Was answer to thy point !—Well fenced !—Well fenc-
    ed !"
Now Heaven forefend it end in death !—He flies !
And from his comrade, the same moment, hath
Our master jerked his sword.—The day is ours !
Quick may they get a surgeon for their wounds,
And I a cordial for my fluttered spirits.
I vow, I'm nigh to swoon !
    Wal. [*without*, L.) Hoa! Alice! Hoa!
Open the door ! Quick, Alice ! Quick !
    Alice. Anon !
Young joints do take no thought of aged ones,
But ever think them supple as themselves.
    Wal. Alice !
    Alice. [*Opening the door.*] I'm here ! A mercy!—Is
    she dead ?

    Enter WALLER, *bearing* LYDIA, *fainting*, L.

    Wal. No !—She but faints—A chair !—Quick, Alice,
    quick !
Water to bathe her temples. [*Exit Alice*, R.] Such a turn
Did fortune never do me ! Shall I kiss
To life these frozen lips ?—No !—Of her plight
'Twere base to take advantage. [*Alice returns*, R., &c.] All
    is well,
The blood returns.
    Alice. How wondrous fair she is !
    Wal. Thou think'st her so ?—No wonder then should I,
                         [*Aside*
How say you ?—Wondrous fair ?
    Alice. Yes ; wondrous fair !
Harm never come to her !—So sweet a thing
'Twere pity were abused !
    Wal. You think her fair?
    Alice. Ay, marry ! Half so fair were more than match
For fairest she e'er saw mine eyes before !
And what a form ! A foot and instep there !
Vouchers of symmetry ! A little foot

And rising instep, from an ankle arching,
A palm, and that a little one, might span.
   Wal. Who taught thee thus ?
   Alice. Why, who but her, taught thee ?
Thy mother !—Heaven rest her !—Thy good mother !
She could read men and women by their hands
And feet !—And here's a hand !—A fairy palm !
Fingers that taper to the pinky tips,
With nails of rose, like shells of such a hue,
Berimmed with pearl, you pick up on the shore !
Save these the gloss and tint do wear without.
   Wal. Why, how thou talk'st !
   Alice. Did I not tell thee, thus
Thy mother used to talk ? Such hand and foot,
She would say, in man or woman, vouched for nature
High tempered !—soil for sentiment refined ;
Affection tender ; apprehension quick—
Degrees beyond the generality !
There is a marriage finger ! Curse the hand
Would balk it of a ring !
   Wal. She's quite restored.
Leave us !—Why cast'st thou that uneasy look ?
Why linger'st thou ? I'm not alone with her—
My honour's with her, too ! I would not wrong her.
   Alice. And if thou would'st, thou'rt not thy mother's
      son.   [*Exit.* R.
   Wal. You are better ?
   Lydia. Much !—Much !
   Wal. Know you him who durst
Attempt this violence in open day ?
He seemed as he would force thee to his coach,
I saw attending.
   Lydia. Take this letter, sir,
And send the answer—I must needs be go !
   Wal. [*Throws the letter away.*] I read no letter ! Tell
      me, what of him
I saw offend thee ?
   Lydia. He hath often met me,
And by design, I think, upon the street,
And tried to win mine ear, which ne'er he got,
Save only by enforcement. Presents—gifts
Of jewels and of gold to wild amount,

To win an audience, hath he proffered me;
Until, methought, my silence—for my lips
Disdained reply where question was a wrong—
Had wearied him. Oh, Sir! whate'er of life
Remains to me I had foregone, ere proved
The horror of this hour!—and you it is
That have protected me!
   Wal. Oh, speak not on't!
   Lydia. You that have saved me from mine enemy—
   Wal. I pray you to forget it.
   Lydia. From a foe
More dire than he that putteth life in peril—
   Wal. Sweet Lydia, I beseech you, spare me.
   Lydia. No!
I will not spare you.—You have brought me safety,
You whom I fear worse than that baleful foe. [*Rises to go.*
   Wal. [*Kneeling and snatching her hand.*] Lydia!
   Lydia. Now make thy bounty perfect. Drop
My hand. That posture, which dishonours thee,
Quit!—for 'tis shame on shame to show respect
Where we do feel disdain. Throw ope thy gate
And let me pass, and never seek with me,
By look, or speech, or aught, communion more!
   Wal. Thou said'st thou lov'dst me!
   Lydia. Yes! when I believed
My tongue did take of thee its last adieu,
And now that I do know it—for be sure,
It never bids adieu to thee again—
Again I tell it thee! Release me, sir!
Rise!—and no hindrance to my will oppose,
That would be free to go.
   Wal. I cannot lose thee!
   Lydia. Thou canst not have me!
   Wal. No!
   Lydia. Thou canst not. I
Repeat it.—Yet I'm thine—thine every way,
Except where honour fences!—Honour, sir,
Not property of gentle blood alone;
Of gentle blood not always property.
Thou'lt not obey me! Still enforcest me!
Oh, what a contradiction is a man!
What in another he one moment spurns,
The next—he does himself complacently!

Wal. Would'st have me lose the hand that holds **my**
   life ?

Lydia. Hear me and keep it, if thou art a man !
I love thee,—for thy benefit would give
The labour of that hand !—wear out my feet !
Rack the invention of my mind ! the powers
Of my heart in one volition gather up !
My life expend, and think no more I gave,
Than he who wins a priceless gem for thanks !
For such good will canst thou return me wrong ?

Wal. Yet, for a while, I cannot let thee go.
Propound for me an oath that I'll not wrong thee ;
An oath which, if I break it, doth entail
Forfeit of earth and heaven.   I'll take it—so
Thou stay'st one hour with me.

Lydia. No !—Not one moment !
Unhand me, or I shriek !—I know the summons
Will pierce into the street, and set me free !
I stand in peril while I'm near thee !   She
Who knows her danger, and delays escape,
Hath but herself to thank, whate'er befals !
Sir, I **may** have a woman's weakness, **but**
i have a woman's resolution, **too,**
And that's a woman's strength !   One moment more !—

Wal. Lo !   Thou art free to go !
      [*Rises, and throws himself distractedly into a chair
      Lydia approaches the door—her pace slackens—she
      pauses with her hand upon the lock—turns and looks
      earnestly on Waller.*

Lydia. (L.) I have a word
To say to thee ; if by thy mother's honour
Thou swear'st to me thou wilt not quit thy seat.

Wal. I swear as thou propound'st to me.

Lydia. [*After a pause, bursting into tears.*] Oh, why—
Why have you used me thus ?   See what you've done !
Essayed to light a guilty passion up,
And kindled in its stead a holy one !
For I do love thee ! (c.) Know'st thou not the wish
To find desert doth bring it oft to sight,
Where yet it is not ? so for substance passes
What only is a phantasm of our minds !
I feared thy love was guilty—yet my wish

To find it honest, stronger than my fear
My fear with fatal triumph overthrew !
Now hope and fear give up to certainty
And I must fly thee—yet must ove thee still
    Wal. Lydia ! By all—
    Lydia. I pray you, hear me out !
Was't right ? was't generous ? was't pitiful ?
One way or other I might be undone :
To love with sin—or love without a hope !
    Wal. Yet hear me, Lydia !—
    Lydia. Stop ! I am undone !
A maid without a heart—robbed of the soil
Wherein life's hopes and wishes root and spring,
And thou the spoiler did me so much hate,
And vowed me so much love !—But I forgive thee !
Yea, I do bless thee ! [*Rushing up and sinking at his feet*
Recollect thy oath !—
Or in thy heart lodged never germ of honour,
But 'tis a desert all !   [*Kisses his hand—presses it to her*
    heart, and kisses it again.
Farewell, then, to thee !   [*Rises.*
May'st thou be happy !   ʳ*Going*
    Wal. Would'st ensure the thing
Thou wishest ?   [*She moves towards the door with a ges*
    ture that prohibits further converse.
Stop !   [*She continues to move on.*
Oh, sternly resolute !   [*She still moves.*
I mean thee honour ! [*She stops and turns towards him.*
    Thou dost meditate—
I know it—flight.—Give me some pause for thought,
But to confirm a mind almost made up.
If in an hour thou hear'st not from me, then
Think me a friend far better lost than won !
Wilt thou do this ?
    Lydia. I will.
    Wal. An hour decides !   [*Exeunt severally.*

    Scene II.—*A Room in Sir William Fondlove's.*

    Enter Trueworth *and* Wildrake, ʀ.
    Wild. You are not angry ?

True. No; I knew the service
I sent you on was one of danger.
   Wild. Thank you.
Most kind you are—And you believe she loves me;
And your own hopes give up to favour mine?
Was ever known such kindness! Much, I fear,
Twill cost you.
   True. Never mind! I'll try and bear it.
   Wild. That's right. No use in yielding to a thing.
Resolve does wonders. Shun the sight of her—
See other women. Fifty to be found
As fair as she.
   True. I doubt it.
   Wild. Doubt it not.
Doubt nothing that gives promise of a cure.
Right handsome dames there are in Lancashire,
Whence called their women witches!—witching things!—
I know a dozen families in which
You'd meet a courtesy worthy of a bow.
I'll give you letters to them.
   True. (L. C.) Will you?
   Wild. (R. C.) Yes.
   True. The worth of a disinterested friend!
   Wild. Oh, Master Trueworth, deeply I'm your debtor!
I own I die for love of neighbour Constance!
And thou to give her up for me! Kind friend!
What won't I do for thee!—Don't pine to death;
I'll find thee fifty ways to cure thy passion,
And make thee heart-whole, if thou'rt so resolved.
Thou shalt be master of my sporting stud,
And go a hunting. If that likes thee not,
Take up thy quarters at my shooting lodge;
There is a cellar to't, make free with it:
I'll thank thee if thou emptiest it. The song
Gives out that wine feeds love—it drowns it, man!
If thou wilt neither hunt nor shoot, try games;
Play at loggats, bowls, fives, dominos, draughts, cribbage,
Backgammon—special recipes for love!
And you believe, for all the hate she shows,
That neighbour Constance loves me?
   True. 'Tis my thought.
   Wild. How shall I find it out?

True. **Affect** to love
Another. Say your passion thrives; the day
Is fixed; and pray her undertake the part
Of bridemaid to your bride. 'Twill bring her out.
  Wild You think she'll own her passion?
  True. If she loves.
  Wild. I thank thee! I will try it! Master Trueworth,
What shall I say to thee, to give her up,
And love her so?
  True. Say nothing.
  Wild. Noble friend!
Kind friend! Instruct another man the way
To win thy mistress! Thou'lt not break thy heart?
Take my advice, thou shalt not be in love
A month! Frequent the play-house!—walk the Parks!
I'll think of fifty ladies that I know,
Yet can't remember now—enchanting ones!
And then there's Lancashire!—and I have friends
In Berkshire and in Wiltshire, that have swarms
Of daughters! Then my shooting lodge and stud!
I'll cure thee in a fortnight of thy love!
And now to neighbor Constance—[*Crosses, L.*]—yet almost
I fear accosting her—a hundred times
Have I essayed to break my mind to her,
But still she stops my mouth with restless scorn!
Howe'er, thy scheme I'll try, and may it thrive!
For I am sick for love of neighbour Constance.
Farewell, dear Master Trueworth! Take my counsel-
Conquer thy passion! Do so! Be a man! [*Exit,* L
  True. Feat easy done that does not tax ourselves!

Enter PHŒBE, R.

  Phœbe. A letter, sir. [*Exit,* R.
  True. Good sooth, a roaming one!
And yet slow traveller. This should have reached me
In Lombardy.—" The hand! Give way, weak seal,
" Thy feeble let too strong for my impatience!"
Ha! Wronged!—Let me contain myself!—Compelled
To fly the roof that gave her birth!—My sister!
No partner in her flight but her pure honour!
I am again a brother.—Pillow, board,
  know not till I find her.

Enter WALLER, R.

Wal. Master Trueworth!

True. Ha! Master Waller! Welcome, Master Waller?

Wal. Good Master Trueworth, thank you. Finding you
From home, I e'en made bold to follow you,
For I esteem you as a man, and fain
Would benefit by your kind offices.
But let me tell you first, to your reproof
I am indebted more than e'er I was
To praise of any other. I am come, sir,
To give you evidence I am not one
Who owns advice is right, and acts not on't.

True. Pray you, explain.

Wal. Will you the bearer be
Of this to one has cause to thank you, too,
Though I the larger debtor?—Read it, sir.

True. [*Reading the letter.*] "At morn to-morrow I will
    make you mine.'
Will you accept from me the name of wife—
The name of husband give me in exchange?"

Wal. How say you, sir?

True. 'Tis boldly—nobly done!

Wal. If she consents—which affectation 'twere
To say I don't—bid her prepare for church,
And you shall act the father, sir, to her
You did the brother by.

True. Right willingly,
Though matter of high moment I defer,
Mind, heart, and soul, are all enlisted in!

Wal. May I implore you, haste! A time is set!--
How light an act of duty makes the heart!

[*Exeunt together,* R

SCENE III.—*Another Chamber in Sir William's House.*

CONSTANCE *discovered,* C

Con. I'll pine to death for no man! Wise it were,
Indeed, to die for neighbour Wildrake—No!—
I know the duty of a woman better—
What fits a maid of spirit! I am out
Of patience with myself, to cast a thought
Away upon him. Hang him! Lovers cost

Naught but the pains of living. I'll get fifty,
And break the heart of every one of them!
I will! I'll be the champion of my sex,
And take revenge on shallow fickle man,
Who gives his heart to fools, and slights the worth
Of proper women! I suppose she's handsome!
My face 'gainst hers at hazard of mine eyes!
A maid of mind! I'll talk her to a stand,
Or tie my tongue for life! A maid of soul!
An artful, managing, dissembling one!
Or she had never caught him—he's no man
To fall in love himself, or long ago,
I warrant, he had fallen in love with me!
I hate the fool—I do. Ha, here he comes!
What brings him hither? Let me dry my eyes;
He must not see I have been crying. Hang him,
I 've much to do, indeed, to cry for him!

Enter WILDRAKE, L.

Wild. Your servant, neighbour Constance.
Con. Servant, sir!
Now what, I wonder, comes the fool to say,
Makes him look so important!
Wild. Neighbour Constance,
I am a happy man.
Con. What makes you so?
Wild. A thriving suit.
Con. In Chancery?
Wild. Oh, no!
In love.
Con. Oh, true! You are in love! Go on!
Wild. Well, as I said, my suit's a thriving one.
Con. You mean you are beloved again?—I don't
Believe it.
Wild. I can give you proof.
Con. What proof?
Love-letters? She's a shameless maid
To write them! Can she spell? Ay, I suppose
With prompting of a dictionary!
Wild. Nay,
Without one.
Con. I will lay you ten to one
She cannot spell! How know you she can spell!

You cannot spell yourself! You write command
With a single M——C—O—M—A—N—D :
Yours to Co-mand.
   Wild. I did not say she wrote
Love-letters to me.
   Con. Then she suffers you to press
Her hand, perhaps?
   Wild. She does.
   Con. Does she press yours!
   Wild. She does.—It goes on swimmingly!   [*Aside*
   Con. She does!
She is no modest woman! I'll be bound,
Your arm the madam suffers round her waist?
   Wild. She does!
   Con. She does! Outrageous forwardness!
Does she let you kiss her?
   Wild. Yes.
   Con. She should be—
   Wild. What?
   Con. What you got thrice your share of when at school,
And yet not half your due! A brazen face!
More could not grant a maid about to wed.
   Wild. She is so.
   Con. What?
   Wild. How swimmingly it goes!   [*Aside.*
   Con. [*with suppressed impatience.*] Are you about to
     marry, neighbour Wildrake?
Are you about to marry?
   Wild. Excellent.   [*Aside.*
   Con. [*Breaking out.*] Why don't you answer me?
   Wild. I am.
   Con. You are—
I tell you what, sir—You're a fool!
   Wild. For what?
   Con. You are not fit to marry! Do not know
Enough of the world, sir! Have no more experience,
Thought, judgment, than a school-boy! Have no mind
Of your own—your wife will make a fool of you,
Will jilt you, break your heart. I wish she may,
I do! You have no more business with a wife
Than I have. Do you mean to say indeed,
You are about to marry?

Wild. Yes, indeed
Con. And when ?
Wild. I'll say to-morrow !   *Aside*
Con. When, I say ?
Wild. To-morrow.
Con. Thank you : much beholden to you !
You've told me on't in time !   I'm very much
Beholden to you, neighbour Wildrake !   And,
I pray you, at what hour ?
  Wild. That we have left
For you to name.
    Con. For me !
    Wild. For you.
    Con. Indeed,
You're very bountiful.   I should not wonder,
Meant you I should be bridesmaid to the lady ?
    Wild. 'Tis just the thing I mean.
    Con. [*Furiously.*] The thing you mean !
Now pray you, neighbour, tell me that again,
And think before you speak ; for much I doubt
You know what you are saying.   Do you mean
To ask me to be bridesmaid ?
    Wild. Even so.
    Con. Bridesmaid ?
    Wild. Ay, bridesmaid !—It is coming fast
Unto a head.   [*Aside.*
    Con. And 'tis for me you wait
To fix the day ?   It shall be doomsday, then !
    Wild. Be doomsday ?
    Con. Doomsday !
    Wild. Wherefore doomsday ?
    Con. [*Boxes him.*] Wherefore !—
Go ask your bride, and give her that from me.
Look, neighbour Wildrake ! you may think this strange,
But don't misconstrue it !   For you are vain, Sir !
And may put down for love what comes from hate.
I should not wonder, thought you I was jealous ;
But I'm not jealous, sir !—would not be so,
Where it was worth my while—I pray henceforth
We may be strangers, sir—you will oblige me
By going out of town—I should not like
To meet you on the street, sir.   Marry, sir !

Marry to-day!   The sooner, sir, the better.
And may you find you have made a bargain, sir
As for the lady!—much I wish her joy.
I pray you, send to me no bride-cake, sir!
Nor gloves—If you do, I'll give them to my maid
Or throw them into the kennel—or the fire.
I am your most obedient servant, sir! |*Exit* ⟨⟩
    Wild. She is a riddle, solve her he who can! [*Exit* ⟨⟩

END OF ACT IV

ACT V.

SCENE I.—*A Room in Sir William's.*

SIR WILLIAM *seated with two* LAWYERS, *discovered.*

Sir W. How many words you take to tell few things
Again,—again say over that, said once,
Methinks, were told enough.
    1st Law. It is the law,
Which labours at precision.
    Sir W. Yes; and thrives
Upon uncertainty—and makes it, too,
With all its pains to shun it.   I could bind
Myself, methinks, with but the twentieth part
Of all this cordage, sirs.—But every man,
As they say, to his own business.   You think
The settlement is handsome ?
    1st Law. Very, sir.
    Sir W. Then now, sirs, we have done, and take ⟨⟩
        thanks,
Which, with your charges, I will render you
Again to-morrow.
    1st Law. Happy nuptials, sir!   [*Exeunt Lawyers,* ⟨⟩
    Sir W. Who passes there ?   Hoa! send my daughter
        to me,
And Master Wildrake, too!   I wait for them.
Bold work!—without her leave to wait upon her,
And ask her go to church !—'Tis taking her
By storm.   What else could move her yesterday,

But jealousy ? What causeth jealousy
But love ? She's mine the moment she receives
Conclusive proof like this, that heart and soul,
And mind and person, I am all her own !
Heigh ho ! These soft alarms are very sweet,
And yet tormenting, too ! Ha ! Master Wildrake,

Enter WILDRAKE, L.

I am glad you're ready, for I'm all in arms
To bear the widow off. Come ! Don't be sad;
All must go merrily, you know, to-day !—
She still doth bear him hard, I see ! The girl
Affects him not, and Trueworth is at fault,
Though clear it is that he doth die for her.   [*Aside.*
Well, daughter—So I see you're ready, too.

Enter CONSTANCE, R.

Why, what's amiss with thee ?

Enter PHŒBE, L.

Phœbe. The coach is here.   [*Exit,* L
Sir W. Come, Wildrake, offer her your arm.
Con. [*To Wildrake.*] I thank you !
I 'm not an invalid !—can use my limbs !
He knows not how to make an arm befits
A lady lean upon.
      Sir W. Why, teach him, then.
      Con. Teach him ! Teach Master Wildrake ! Teach,
            indeed !
I taught my dog to beg, because I knew
That he could learn it.
      Sir W. Peace, thou little shrew !
I'll have no wrangling on my wedding-day !
Here, take my arm.
      Con. I'll not !—I'll walk alone !   [*Crosses,* L.
Live, die alone ! I do abominate
The fool and all his sex !
      Sir W. Again !
      Con. I have done.
When do you marry, Master Wildrake ? She
Will want a husband goes to church with thee ! [*Exeunt,* L

SCENE II.—*Widow Green's Dressing Room.*

WIDOW GREEN *discovered at her Toilet, attended by* AMELIA
— *Waller's letter to Lydia in her hand.*

Widow G. Oh, bond of destiny!—Fair bond, that scal'st
My fate in happiness!—I'll read thee yet
Again—although thou'rt written on my heart.
But here his hand, inditing thee, did lie!
And this the tracing of his fingers! So
I read thee that could rhyme thee, as my prayers!
" *At noon to-morrow will I make thee mine,*
Wilt thou receive from me the name of wife—
The name of husband give me in exchange?"
The traitress! to break ope my billet-doux,
And take the envelope!—But I forgive her,
Since she did leave the rich contents behind
Amelia, give this feather more a slope,
That it sit droopingly. I would look all
Dissolvement, naught about me to bespeak
Boldness! I would appear a timid bride,
Trembling upon the verge of wifehood, as
I ne'er before had stood there! That will do.
Oh, dear!—how I am agitated—don't   .
I look so? I have found a secret out.
Nothing in women strikes a man so much
As to look interesting! Hang this cheek
Of mine! It is too saucy; what a pity
To have a colour of one's own!—Amelia!
Could you contrive, dear girl, to bleach my cheek,
How I would thank you! I could give it then
What tint I chose, and that should be the hectic
Bespeaks a heart in delicate commotion.
I am much too florid : stick a rose in my hair,
The brightest you can find; 'twill help, my girl,
Subdue my rebel colour—Nay, the rose
Doth lose complexion, not my cheek! Exchange it
For a carnation. That's the flower, Amelia!
You see how it doth triumph o'er my cheek.
Are you content with me?
    Amel. I am, my lady.
    Widow G. And whither, think you, has the hussy gone

Whose place you fill so well ?--Into the country !
Or fancy you she stops in town ?
  Amel. I can't
Conjecture.
  Widow G. Shame upon her ! Leave her place
Without a moment's warning—with a man, too ;
Seemed he a gentleman that took her hence ?
  Amel. He did.
  Widow G. You never saw him here before ?
  Amel. Never.
  Widow G. Not lounging on the other side
Of the street, and reconnoitering the windows ?
  Amel. Never.
  Widow G. 'Twas planned by letter. Notes, you know
Have often come to her—But I forgive her,
Since this advice she chanced to leave behind
Of gentle Master Waller's wishes, which
I bless myself in blessing !—[*A knock.*] Gods, a knock !
'Tis he ! Show in those ladies are so kind
To act my bridesmaids for me, on this brief
And agitating notice. [*Amelia goes out, R.*] Yes, I look
A bride sufficiently ! And this the hand
That gives away my liberty again ?
Upon my life it is a pretty hand,
A delicate and sentimental hand !
No lotion equals gloves ; no woman knows
The use of them that does not sleep in them !
My neck hath kept its colour wondrously
Well ; after all, it is no miracle
That I should win the heart of a young man.
My bridesmaids come, Oh, dear !

        Enter two LADIES, R.

  1st Lady. How do you ? A good morning to you—
      Poor dear,
How much you are affected ! Why, we thought
You ne'er would summon us.
  Widow G. One takes, you know,
When one is flurried, twice the time to dress.
My dears, has either of you salts ! I thank you !
They are excellent ; the virtue's gone from mine,
Nor thought I of renewing them.—Indeed,
I'm unprovided quite for this affair

1st Lady. I think the bridegroom's come !

Widow G. Don't say so ! How
You've made my heart jump !

1st Lady. As you sent for us,
A new-launched carriage drove up to the door ;
The servants all in favours.

Widow G. 'Pon my life,
I never shall get through it ; lend me your hand.
[*Half rises and throws herself back on her chair again.*
I must sit down again ! There came just now
A feeling like to swooning over me.
I'm sure, before 'tis over, I shall make
A fool of myself ! I vow, I thought not half
So much of my first wedding-day ! I'll make
An effort. Let me lean upon your arm,
And give me yours, my dear. Amelia, mind
Keep near me with the smelling bottle.

Enter SERVANT, R.

Ser. Madam,
The bridegroom's come.   [*Exit,* R.

Widow G. The brute has knocked me down !
To bolt it out so ! I had started less
If he had fired a cannon at my ear.
How shall I ever manage to hold up
Till all is done ! I'm tremor head to foot.
You can excuse me, can't you ? Pity me.
One may feel queer upon one's wedding-day. [*Exeunt,* R

SCENE III.—*A Drawing-Room.*

Enter SERVANTS, R., *showing in* S R WILLIAM FONDLOVE,
CONSTANCE, *and* WILDRAKE,— *Servants exeunt,* C.

Sir W. [*Aside to Wildrake.*] Good Master Wildrake
look more cheerfully !—Come,
You do not honour to my wedding-day.
How brisk am I ? My body moves on springs !
My stature gives no inch I throw away ;
My supple joints play free and sportfully ;
I'm every atom what a man should be.

Wild. I pray you, pardon me, Sir William !

Sir W. Smile, then,

And talk, and rally me! I did expect
Ere half an hour had passed, you would have put me
A dozen times to the blush. Without such things,
A bridegroom knows not his own wedding-day.
I see! Her looks are glossary to thine:
She flouts thee still,—I marvel not at thee;
There's thunder in that cloud! I would to-day
It would disperse, and gather in the morning.
I fear me much, thou know'st not how to woo.
I'll give thee a lesson. Ever there's a way,
But knows one how to take it! Twenty men
Have courted Widow Green. Who has her now?
I sent to advertise her, that to-day
I meant to marry her. She would not open
My note. And gave I up? I took the way
To make her love me! I did send again,
To pray her leave my daughter should be bridesmaid
That letter, too, came back. Did I give up?
I took the way to make her love me! Yet
Again I sent to ask what church she chose
To marry at; my note came back again;
And did I yet give up? I took the way
To make her love me. All the while, I found
She was preparing for the wedding. Take
A hint from me! She comes! My fluttering heart
Gives note the empress of its realms is near.
Now, Master Wildrake, mark and learn from me
How it behoves a bridegroom play his part.

Enter WIDOW GREEN, L., *supported by her Bridesmade
and followed by* AMELIA.

Widow G. I cannot raise my eyes—they cannot bear
The beams of his, which, like the sun's, I feel
Are on me, though I see them not, enlightening
The heaven of his young face; nor dare I scan
The brightness of his form, which symmetry,
And youth and beauty, in enriching vie.
He kneels to me! Now grows my breathing thick,   -
As though I did await a seraph's voice,
Too rich for mortal ear.
   Sir W. My gentle bride!
   Widow G. Who's that? who speaks to me?
  F

Sir W. These transports check.
Lo, an example to mankind I set,
Of amorous emprise ; and who should thrive
In love, if not Love's soldier, who doth press
The doubtful siege, and will not own repulse.
Lo ! here I tender thee my fealty,
To live thy duteous slave. My queen thou art,
In frowns or smiles, to give me life or death.
Oh, deign look down upon me ! In thy face
Alone I look on day ; it is my sun
Most bright ; the which denied, no sun doth rise.
Shine out upon me, my divinity !
My gentle Widow Green ! my wife to be !
My love, my life, my drooping, blushing bride !
    Widow G. (R. C.) Sir William Fondlove, you're a fool !
    Sir W. (L. C.) A fool ?
    Widow G. Why come you hither, sir, in trim like this !
Or rather, why at all ?
    Sir W. Why come I hither ?
To marry thee !
    Widow G. The man will drive me mad !
Sir William Fondlove, I'm but forty, sir,
And you are sixty, seventy, if a day ;
At least you look it, sir. I marry you !
When did a woman wed her grandfather ?
    Sir W. Her brain is turned !
    Widow G. You're in your dotage, sir,
And yet a boy in vanity ! But know
Yourself from me : you're old and ugly, sir.
    Sir W. Do you deny you are in love with me ?
    Widow G. In love with thee !
    Sir W. That you are jealous of me ?
    Widow G. Jealous !
    Sir W. To very lunacy ?
    Widow G. To hear him !
    Sir W. Do you forget what happened yesterday ?
    Widow G. Sir William Fondlove !—   [*Crosses,* L.
    Sir W. (R.) Widow Green, fair play !—
Are you not laughing ? Is it not a jest ?
Do you believe me seventy to a day ?
Do I look it ? Am I old and ugly ? Why,
Why do I see those favours in the hall,

These ladies dressed as bridesmaids, thee as bride,
Unless to marry me ?　　　　　　　　　　*[Knock.*
Widow G. He is coming, sir,
Shall answer you for me !

　　Enter WALLER, L., *with Gentlemen as Bridesmen.*

Wal. Where is she ?　What !
All that bespeaks the day, except the fair
That's queen of it ?　Most kind of you to grace
My nuptial so !　But that I render you
My thanks in full, make full my happiness,
And tell me where's my bride ?
Widow G. She's here.
Wal. Where ?
Widow G. Here,
Fair Master Waller !
Wal. Lady, do not mock me.
Widow G. Mock thee !　My heart is stranger to such
　　mood ;
'Tis serious tenderness and duty all.
I pray you, mock not me, for I do strive
With fears and soft emotions, that require
Support.　Take not away my little strength,
And leave me at the mercy of a feather.
I am thy bride !　If 'tis thy happiness
To think me so, believe it, and be rich
To thy most boundless wishes.　Master Waller.
I am thy waiting bride, the Widow Green !
Wal. Lady, no widow is the bride I seek,
But one the church has never given yet
The nuptial blessing to !
Widow G. What mean you, sir ?
Why come a bridegroom here, if not to me
You sued to be your bride ?　Is this your hand, sir ?
　　　　　　　　　　　　　　[Showing letter.
Wal. It is ! addressed to your fair waiting maid.
Widow G. My waiting-maid !　The laugh is passing
　　round,
And now the turn is yours, sir.　She is gone
Eloped ! run off ! and with the gentleman
That brought your billet-doux.
Wal. Is Trueworth false ?

He must be false.   What madness tempted me
To trust him with such audience as I know
Must sense, and mind, and soul of man entrance,
And leave him but the power to feel its spell !
Of his own lesson he would profit take,
And plead at once an honorable love,
Supplanting mine, less pure, reformed too late !
And if he did, what merit I, except
To lose the maid I would have wrongly won,
And, had I rightly prized her, now had worn ?
I get but my deservings !

Enter TRUEWORTH, R. C., *leading in* LYDIA *richly dressed,
and veiled from head to foot.*

Master Trueworth,   -
Though for thy treachery thou hast excuse,
Thou must account for it, so much I lose !
Sir, you have wronged me to amount beyond
Acres, and gold, and life, which makes them rich.
And compensation I demand of you,
Such as a man expects, and none but one
That's less than man refuses.   Where's the maid
You falsely did abstract ?
   True. I took her hence.
But not by guile, nor yet enforcement, sir,
But of her free will, knowing what she did.
" That, as I found I cannot give her back,
" I own her state is changed, but in her place
" This maid I offer you, her image, far
" As feature, form, complexion, nature go .
" Resemblance halting only there, where thou
" Thyself didst pause—condition ; for this maid
" Is gently born and generously bred."
Lo ! for your fair loss, fair equivalent !
   Wal. Show me another sun, another earth.
I can inhabit, as this Sun and Earth ;
As thou did'st take the maid, the maid herself
Give back herself, her sole equivalent !
   True. Her sole equivalent I offer you !
My sister, sir, long counted lost, now found,
Who fled her home unwelcome bands to 'scape
" Which a half-father would have forced upon her.

" Taking advantage of her brother's absence
" Away on travel in a distant land !
' Returned, I missed her ; of the cause received
' Invention, coward, false and criminating !
' And gave her up for lost, but happily
' Did find her yesterday"—Behold her, sir ! [*Removes veil.*
  Wal. Lydia !
  Widow G. My waiting-maid !
  Wal. Thy sister, Trueworth !
Art thou fit brother to this virtuous maid ?
  True. [*Giving Lydia to Waller.*] Let this assure thee.
  Lydia. [*Crosses* R.—*To Widow Green.*] Madam, pardon
    me
My double character, for honesty—
No other end—assumed, and my concealment
Of Master Waller's love.   In all things else,
I trust I may believe you hold me blameless ;
At least, I'll say for you I should be so,
For it was pastime, madam, not a task,
To wait upon you!   Little you exacted,
And ever made the most of what I did
In mere obedience to you.
  Widow G. Give me your hand ;
No love without a little roguery.
If you do play the mistress well as maid,
You will bear off the bell !   There never was
A better girl ! [*Waller and Lydia go up.*] I have made
    myself a fool ;
I am undone, if goes the news abroad,
My wedding-dress I donned for no effect,
Except to put it off !   I must be married.
I'm a lost woman, if another day
I go without a husband !—What a sight
He looks by Master Waller !—Yet he is physic
I die without, so needs must gulp it down.
I'll swallow him with what good grace I can.
Sir William Fondlove !
  Sir W. Widow Green !
  Widow G. I own
I have been rude to you.   Thou dost not look
So old by thirty, forty years, as I
Did say.   Thou'rt far from ugly—very far

And as I said, Sir William, once before,
Thou art a kind and right good-humoured man:
I was but angry with you! Why, I'll tell you
At more convenient season—and you know
An angry woman heeds not what she says,
And will say anything!

 Sir W. I were unworthy
The name of man, if an apology
So gracious came off profitless, and from
A lady! Will you take me, Widow Green?

 Widow G. Hem!   {*Courtesies.*

 True. [*To Wildrake.*] Master Wildrake dressed to go
  to church!
She has acknowledged, then, she loves thee?—No?
Give me thy hand, I'll lead thee up to her.

 Wild. 'Sdeath! what are you about? You know her
  not.
She'll brain thee!

 True. Fear not: come along with me.
Fair Mistress Constance!

 Con. Well, sir!

 Wild. [*To Trueworth.*] Mind!

 True. Don't fear.
Love you not neighbour Wildrake?

 Con. Love, sir!

 True. Yes,
You do.

 Con. He loves another, sir, he does!
I hate him. We were children, sir, together
For fifteen years and more; there never came
The day we did not quarrel, make it up,
Quarrel again, and make it up again:
Were never neighbours more like neighbours, sir
Since he became a man, and I a woman,
It still has been the same; nor cared I ever
To give a frown to any other, sir.
And now to come and tell me he's in love,
And ask me to be bridesmaid to his bride!
How durst he do it, sir!—to fall in love!
Methinks at least he might have asked my leave
Nor had I wondered had he asked myself, sir!

 Wild. Then give thyself to me!

Con. How! what!

Wild. Be mine!
Thou art the only maid thy neighbour loves.

   Con. Art serious, neighbour Wildrake?

   Wild. In the church   ·
I'll answer thee, if thou wilt take me; though
I neither dress, nor walk, nor dance, nor know
" The Widow Jones" from an Italian, French,
Or German air.

   Con. No more of that.—My hand.

   Wild. Giv'st it as free as thou didst yesterday?

   Con. [*Affecting to strike him.*] Nay!

   Wild. I will thank it, give it how thou wilt.

   Widow G. A triple wedding! May the Widow Green
Obtain brief hearing e'er she quits the scene,
The Love-Chase to your kindness to commend,
In favour of an old, now absent friend!

THE END.